W9-BZK-203

ALSO BY SHARON M. DRAPER

Copper Sun
Double Dutch
Out of My Mind
Panic
Romiette & Julio

The Jericho Trilogy:
The Battle of Jericho
November Blues
Just Another Hero

The Hazelwood High Trilogy:
Tears of a Tiger
Forged by Fire
Darkness Before Dawn

Clubhouse Mysteries
The Buried Bones Mystery
Lost in the Tunnel of Time
Shadows of Caesar's Creek
The Space Mission Adventure
The Backyard Animal Show
Stars and Sparks on Stage

STELLA by STARLIGHT

STELLA by STARLIGHT

SHARON M. DRAPER

Atheneum
Atheneum Books for Young Readers
New York London Toronto Sydney New Delhi

ATHENEUM BOOKS FOR YOUNG READERS
An imprint of Simon & Schuster Children's Publishing Division
1230 Avenue of the Americas, New York, New York 10020

This book is a work of fiction. Any references to historical events, real people, or real places are used fictitiously. Other names, characters, places, and events are products of the author's imagination, and any resemblance to actual events or places or persons, living or dead, is entirely coincidental.

Text copyright © 2015 by Sharon M. Draper
Jacket illustration copyright © 2015 by Sarah Jane Coleman
All rights reserved, including the right of reproduction in whole or in part in any form.

ATHENEUM BOOKS FOR YOUNG READERS is a registered trademark of Simon & Schuster, Inc.
Atheneum logo is a trademark of Simon & Schuster, Inc.
For information about special discounts for bulk purchases, please contact Simon & Schuster Special Sales at 1-866-506-1949 or business@simonandschuster.com.
The Simon & Schuster Speakers Bureau can bring authors to your live event. For more information or to book an event, contact the Simon & Schuster Speakers Bureau at 1-866-248-3049 or visit our website at www.simonspeakers.com.
Book design by Debra Sfetsios-Conover and Irene Metaxatos
The text for this book is set in Scala OT.
1015 FFG
Manufactured in the United States of America

10 9 8 7 6 5
Library of Congress Cataloging-in-Publication Data
Draper, Sharon M. (Sharon Mills)
Stella by starlight / Sharon Draper.
pages cm
Summary: When a burning cross set by the Klan causes panic and fear in 1932 Bumblebee, North Carolina, fifth-grader Stella must face prejudice and find the strength to demand change in her segregated town.
ISBN 978-1-4424-9497-8 (hardcover)
ISBN 978-1-4424-9499-2 (eBook)
[1. Prejudices—Fiction. 2. Segregation—Fiction. 3. Civil rights—Fiction. 4. African Americans—Fiction. 5. Ku Klux Klan (1915-)—Fiction. 6. North Carolina—History—20th century—Fiction.] I. Title.
PZ7.D78325Su 2015
[Fic]—dc23
2014038728

This book is dedicated to my father, Vick D. Mills.
He is my hero and will forever have my heart.
I promised him so long ago that I would write this story.
I wrote this for you, Daddy.
I'm sorry it took so long.

As a boy, he walked those dusty North Carolina roads, exulted in the
beauty of the land, and basked in the love of his mother, Estelle.
He feasted on her homegrown, home-cooked meals, as well as her wisdom.
He also listened to the stories of the elders, grew strong from the love of family and
community, and learned to face with dignity the sometimes harsh realities of life.

So this book is also dedicated to my grandmother, Estelle Twitty Mills Davis.
She lived from 1905 to 1983.
She, too, listened to the elders and learned to survive pain.
Her life was not always easy, and she struggled with many things.
But she loved her children and she passed her strength along to them.
And she kept her memories in that journal.

So this is Estelle's tale and Vick's tale combined.
It is a gift of love.

STELLA by STARLIGHT

✳1✳
Flames Across the Water

Nine robed figures dressed all in white. Heads covered with softly pointed hoods. Against the black of night, a single wooden cross blazed. Reflections of peppery-red flames shimmered across the otherwise dark surface of Kilkenny Pond.

Two children, crouched behind the low-hanging branches of a hulking oak tree on the other side of the pond, watched the flickers of scarlet in the distance in fearful silence. Dressed only in nightshirts, Stella Mills and her brother Jojo shivered in the midnight October chill.

Stella yanked the boy close, dry leaves crunching beneath his bare feet. "Shh!" she whispered, holding him tightly. "Don't move!"

Jojo squirmed out of her grasp. "It was *me* that saw 'em first!" he protested. "You'd still be 'sleep if I hadn't come and got you. So lemme see!"

Stella covered her brother's lips with her fingers to quiet him. Even though her toes were numb with cold and she knew they needed to get out of there, she could not take her eyes from the horror glimmering toward them from across the pond. "Do you *know* what would happen if they saw us?" she whispered, shifting her stinging feet, the crushing of dry leaves seeming far too loud.

Jojo pressed himself closer to her in answer.

Besides the traitorous leaves, Stella could hear a pair of bullfrogs *ba-rupping* to each other, but nothing, not a single human voice, from across the pond. She could, however, smell the charring pine, tinged with . . . what? She sniffed deeper—it was acrid, harsh. Kerosene. A trail of gray smoke snaked up to the sky, merging with the clouds.

"Who *are* they?" Jojo whispered, stealing another glance.

"The Klan." Just saying those words made Stella's lips quiver.

The Ku Klux Klan.

Here.

Here!

"What are they doing?"

"Practicing, I think."

"For what?"

Stella paused and smoothed his bushy hair, trying to figure out the best way to answer. Jojo was only eight.

"Nothing good," she said at last.

A horse whinnied in the distance—it sounded nervous. And there, in the shadows of the trees across the pond, Stella could make out half a dozen of them. *The flames must be scaring them, too,* she thought. The horses began to stamp and snort as the fire flared.

Stella inched forward, trying to get a better look. One of the harnesses seemed to sparkle in the darkness. Or was it just a stray ember from the flames? The men in the white hoods were now all raising their arms to the sky, and they cried out as one, but their exact words were muffled by cloth and wind.

"Jojo, we've gotta get out of here!" she whispered, now edging backward.

"Should we tell Mama and Papa?" Jojo asked.

Stella did not answer her brother. Instead she caught his hand in her tightest grip and ran.

⋆ 2 ⋆
Swift and Silent

The family sat huddled around the only table in the house, with Dusty, their brindle hound, curled underneath. Stella loved the feel of that table—she loved to trace the circular patterns in the warm brown wood. Made of elm and built by her father when he married her mother, the table was large, sturdy, and dependable—and so much more than a place for meals. It was a sewing table for her mother, a place to clean fish for her father, the battleground for many family games of checkers, and even a pretend track for Jojo to race his two wooden toy cars. Stella, now nervously circling the burl of the wood grain at double speed, thought tonight could be the one when she wore a hole clear through it.

She looked from her mother to her father to her

mother again, telling them for the second time exactly what she and Jojo had seen. Papa had run outside fast as a shot to see for himself as soon as she had awakened him. When he got back, his hands were trembling, his words were short. "Red fire. Black cross. White hoods. They're here. Now," he told Mama.

It was 1932, in the little town of Bumblebee, North Carolina, tucked in the rocky bottom of the Blue Ridge Mountains, miles of stone-clogged farmland and forest all around. Folks on Stella's side of town worked as maids and cooks, janitors and sharecropping farmers. A few lucky men got jobs at the lumber mill, the only real industry in town. But they weren't allowed to handle the saws—only the boards and the sawdust.

Every Negro family in Bumblebee knew the unwritten rules—they had to take care of their own problems and take care of one another. Help from the white community was neither expected nor considered. It was as it always had been.

"Are you sure they didn't see you?" Papa asked again brusquely, rubbing a hand over his unshaven chin.

"No, they didn't, Papa," Stella replied, her finger tracing faster, faster. "I'm sure of it."

"We hid behind a tree," Jojo chimed in. "We're smooth as shadows."

"You're not smooth—you're bordering on stupid!" their mother erupted angrily. "If they'd a spotted you, no tellin' what they would have done!"

"What were you doing up anyway?" Stella thought to ask her brother.

He made a face. "I had to tee-tee. But when I got to the outhouse, I thought I heard voices, and I thought maybe somebody was out having fun, so I peeked around back, saw the fire across the pond." He paused and glanced up at his parents. "So then I got Stella."

Papa banged his fist against the table. "And so *both* of you snuck out to look. . . . Lord a mercy, we are *not* talking about fun or games!"

Stella froze.

Then her father lowered his voice. "My job is to keep you all safe," he said slowly and evenly. "Best way to do that is to stay away from trouble, not bring it to us. You got that?" He fixed a glare on them both.

"Yes, Papa," they said in unison.

"Last time the Klan was active," Mama noted, "was when Billy Odom had what they called the 'accident.'"

Stella's mind raced. *The accident!* Mr. Odom had fallen against a blade down at the lumber mill. She'd been younger than Jojo at the time, but Stella remembered the furtive whispers and the tracings of fear on the grown-ups around her when it had happened.

As if he had read her mind, Papa nodded grimly. "He was gettin' ready to start his own blacksmith shop. Klan made it clear that weren't gonna happen."

"Those men . . . tonight . . . they looked like ghosts," Jojo whispered. "They looked like they might be able to fly or something!"

To Stella, their father's face, etched with worry in the lamp-lit room, was more frightening than any ghosts. This was real. She slipped her foot under the table until it reached Jojo's, and gave his a tap for courage. It gave her courage too, made her brave enough to tell something else that had been gnawing at her.

"Papa," she began.

"What?"

"Uh, some of those men had their horses with them."

Her father leaned toward her. "And . . . ," he prompted.

"I'm not sure, but I think maybe I might have recognized one of the horses. But it was dark, and I was kinda scared, and now that I think about it, I don't really know for sure." She traced a figure eight in the wood.

"What do you think you saw, honey?" her mother asked, reaching across the table to calm Stella's fingers.

"I might have . . . well . . . I might have seen one of the horses before," Stella said.

"At night, one horse looks pretty much like all the others, though, doesn't it?" her father said. "Think now." His voice had taken on a different edge, and Stella felt even more nervous. She pulled her hand away from her mother's.

"It seemed like this horse had a saddle and harness that sparkled—like it was catching the reflection of the flames," Stella said, trying to remember. "It seemed like the other horses didn't stand out. But this one did."

Mama reached out again, this time to tap Papa's hand. "Doc Packard dresses his horses real fine."

Papa cleared his throat. "I know." He stood up and

8

began to pace back and forth, nodding and mumbling as he walked faster and faster. Finally he stopped and looked at them all. "We have this knowledge now, and that gives us a little power. That's about all I got in my back pocket. So in a way, it's good you saw what you saw tonight. But this can be mighty bad. Mighty bad."

He ran his fingers through his thick hair and started back up, walking and thinking, thinking and walking. Then he stopped yet again.

"Stella, you and Jojo come with me. We gotta wake the men down the lane."

"How come?" Jojo asked.

"Because I said so, boy!" Papa was already headed for the door. "I'll take the left side of the road. You two take the right. Tell them we gotta meet. Our house. A half hour. Shake a leg, now."

"And be careful!" Mama admonished. "Swift and silent, you hear me? Take the dog."

Stella and Jojo dressed quickly and dashed out into the night, Dusty padding close behind. Stella could still smell smoke in the distance.

They ran to the Winston house first, pounding on their front door. A few minutes later, Johnsteve, a burly, brown-skinned boy, opened it cautiously. "What y'all doing out here in the middle of the night?" he asked, blinking at them.

"Tell your daddy to get to my house right away," Stella whispered urgently. "There's trouble out by Kilkenny Pond. Klan."

Johnsteve's face shifted from sleepy and annoyed to instantly alert. "I'll tell him!" he said, closing the door in a rush.

Stella and Jojo then ran on to the house of the only Negro doctor in town, Dr. Hawkins, then to the school-teacher's, then to every other right-side house on River-side Road.

Folks reacted almost as quickly as the fire had spread up that cross. Men still tucking their night-shirts into hastily pulled-on overalls hurried down the road, a couple of them carrying shotguns. And in less than half an hour, Stella's front room was filled with the bristling anger of the black men of Bumblebee.

★ 3 ★
Feeling Uneven

While the men talked in heated whispers in the kitchen, Stella and Dr. Hawkins's son, Anthony, sat outside on the front steps. Jojo, very much against his will, had been sent to sleep in his parents' bed in the upstairs loft. Anthony had come with his father, but the children had been told to make themselves scarce, which pretty much was what Stella was usually told when grown-ups started talking grown-up stuff. Most times, that made no never mind to her—their talk was usually pretty dull listening. But this time she was irked. This had to do with *all* of them!

Well, at least Anthony was there. Even though she and Tony were both in the fifth grade and had walked to school together since first grade, Stella felt a little self-conscious sitting in the dark with a boy. She touched her hair. She knew it was a mess, and she wasn't quite sure why that bothered her so much. Plus, it was cold! She'd at least thought to grab a blanket off her bed before she left the house, and now she pulled it, and the dog, closer.

"You ever been outside at three in the morning before?" Stella finally asked Tony, who looked warm in a woolen jacket.

"Lots of times. I usually go with my father when he has an emergency," he replied. "I like the night."

"Me too," Stella said. She looked up at the sky; dusky clouds shifted above, shielding, then revealing, then shielding the stars again.

"Me and Jojo saw the Klan tonight. Burning a cross," she added quietly.

"Yeah. My father told me." He paused, then asked, "Were you scared?"

"My guts felt frozen," Stella admitted.

Tony went silent, as silent as the night. The insects and tree frogs, Stella figured, had tucked themselves into some muddy place, just trying to keep warm. No nighttime animals called to one another—at least none that she could hear. Even Dusty was quiet, folded at her feet, but he sniffed the air, watchful and alert.

"You want to know a secret?" Tony asked out of the blue.

"Sure," Stella said, shrugging, still trying to feel as if sitting outside with a boy at three in the morning was a perfectly normal thing to be doing.

"Sometimes, at night, I go and run at the track of the white school." As Stella gaped, he hurried on. "It's honest-to-goodness cinder, you know? It's so much better than running on our lumpy dirt road. On that white school track, I feel like an eagle or something."

Stella didn't doubt it—Tony was one heck of a runner. None of the boys in the school, not even those taking high school classes, could beat him in a footrace. Still, the white school track! Stella drew in her breath. "You're gonna get in big trouble if they find out."

"I'm too fast! Who's gonna catch me?" Tony said, leaping up, bouncing from step to step. "My legs feel the burn of the run before my body even knows I'm moving!"

In spite of everything, Stella laughed out loud.

Tony stopped jumping and got serious. "I want to be like the Midnight Express."

"What's that—a train?"

"Don't you know the Midnight Express? It's Eddie Tolan. He won two gold medals in track at the Olympics this summer. *World records*, girl! In the hundred-meter and two-hundred-meter events. They even gave him the title 'World's Fastest Human.'" Tony bent his elbows into a running stance. "Tolan was the only colored boy to get golds in track!"

"I had no idea they let colored people be in the Olympics."

"I guess so. I read about him in the *Carolina Times* back in August." Tony began bouncing from step to step again. "I'm gonna run in the Olympics one day," he declared.

"But we don't even have a track team at our school, never mind a place to practice."

"Yeah, but the white school does. That's why I use their track at night."

"You think if you went to that school, they'd let you run on their team?" Stella asked.

Tony's step jumping slowed down. "Probably not."

After a moment Stella said quietly, "You're not the only one with a secret."

"Yeah?"

Stella looked back at the door to make sure it was still closed. "Sometimes I sneak outside real late at night too . . . to write."

"To *write*? But . . . why? We get enough of that in school!"

Stella thought about that for a moment. "Well, I don't like writing much, and I'm not so very good at it, so I practice when nobody is around." *He must think I'm really goofy*, she thought, but Tony was quiet as she tried to explain. "But I *do* like being outside in the darkness. At least I did before tonight. Seems like stuff that's hard for me at school is easier at night. Does that make sense?"

"Yeah, I get it." Tony glanced at the closed door, then lowered his voice. "You gonna write about the Klan?"

Stella's eyes widened. "Oh, I couldn't! What if . . ."

"What if what?"

She hesitated. "I know this sounds crazy, but what if somehow one of them finds out about what I saw? And . . . that's not all. . . ."

"What's not all?"

Stella's heart began to thud. "*Please* don't tell anybody, but I think I know who one of them is."

Tony sat back down in a blink. "That kind of information can get you hurt, girl."

"I know! That's why I am *not* writing about it!" She paused. "Besides, I don't think I could put into words the shiver down my back or the tingle in my toes or the thunder of my heartbeat while we watched."

"You just did," Tony told her matter-of-factly.

Stella shook her head. "Why do you think they were out there tonight? They haven't done anything like this around here for a long time, Papa says."

Tony stared out into the dark. "All I know is every time they get to showing off their pointy bedsheets, something bad happens."

"I got a feeling they like making us feel uneven."

"How you mean?"

"Well, it's sort of like we're living on a boat that might sink."

Tony nodded. "With no oars, and holes in the boat!"

"I think when we get scared, they feel strong," Stella reasoned.

"But . . . why? What's the point?" Tony tilted his

head toward the house. "What do you think the old folks are talking about?"

"They've gotta be worried," Stella said. "Real worried. But not one of them ever *does* anything!" She stomped her foot on the rough wooden step.

"But, Stella, what *can* they do? They got no power. No money. Like *my* daddy says, it's hard to live like there's a boot on your back every second of your life." He reached down for a handful of pebbles and flung them into the night. A clatter immediately followed— he had a good arm as well as being fast—those pebbles had reached the front fence.

"Yeah, but your daddy got out," Stella ventured. "He went to college and now he's a doctor."

Because he was the only Negro doctor for two hundred miles, Tony's father delivered babies, gave tonics and cough medicine for head colds, and patched up scratches, cuts, and burns. He stayed busy seven days a week.

"Yeah, he did. But he's told me more than enough stories about how bad he was treated while he was getting his training. They made him empty the bedpans and clean up the blood on the floor after a surgery.

None of the other interns had to do that. They gave him broken equipment and outdated books, and only let him treat colored folk."

Stella tucked her toes under the edge of her blanket. "My papa always tells me we gotta be twice as smart to get half as much," she told Tony with a frown.

Tony's voice grew tight. "And even after all this time, my daddy's *still* not allowed to treat white patients. Like their diseases are high class or something." He whipped more stones after the first ones. "And Dr. Packard, the white doctor—he won't even lay a hand on a black patient, even if they're dyin'!" he added.

"Oh, he'll lay a hand when he *wants* to." Stella's voice went harsh.

"How do you mean?" Tony asked, wiping his hands on his pants.

"When I was five, Dr. Packard, well, he slapped me—hard—right across my face. I can still remember, it hurt so bad."

"He did? But why?"

"Remember that game, 'Step on a crack, break your mother's back'?"

"Yeah, you jump over the cracks in the sidewalk."

"Well, I was with Mama and we were walking down Main Street, heading to Mrs. Cooper's candy store—I was so happy! I was concentrating on the sidewalk, doing my jumps, and I didn't see Dr. Packard. I accidentally stepped on his shoe and got some mud on it."

Tony sucked in his breath. "You didn't!"

"Yep. I did. I apologized over and over, and so did my mother. She even bent down to wipe off the mud with her handkerchief. But he pushed my mom away—she almost fell—and then he reached down and whomped me as hard as he could. I remember his green eyes as he sneered at me. Then he called me stupid and careless and some other stuff I'm not gonna repeat, and he walked away."

Tony exhaled hard, angry. "Gosh, Stella. So whadja do?"

"I started crying. Worse than that—Mama cried. And there was nothing that either of us could do except go home. And I never did get any candy."

Now *she* grabbed up some of the pebbles and flung them across the yard. No clatter. But the voices inside were getting louder, so maybe she just didn't hear it.

Dusty raised his head and growled softly. "Settle down, settle down, now," Stella whispered, stroking the dog's back. "Everything's gonna be okay, boy."

But she wasn't sure about that at all.

✦ 4 ✦
Nailing Jelly to a Tree

The meeting was breaking up just as Stella decided she and Tony were about to surely freeze to death. She opened the front door hesitantly to the smell of tobacco and sweat and strong coffee. The neighbor men, a good twenty of them, were saying goodbye, clapping one another on the back, making their way out. Roosters had begun crowing up and down the road. No adult would be going back to sleep that morning.

Stella said bye to Tony and grabbed a broom without being told. Sweeping stray ashes from the hearth, beating at the stones, she was so rough that shards of corn husk broke from the broom's bottom.

Her mother took the broom from Stella's hands.

"You been up half the night, honeygirl," she said gently. "Go lie down for an hour before school."

Stella started to protest, but a firm push from her mother changed her mind. Her pillow was pancake flat, so she gave it a shake, plumped it up, and laid her head down, suddenly exhausted. Scooching her knees up, she gazed at the newspaper-covered wall next to her bed. Most every plank of pine wood inside the house was covered with old newspapers. Newsy decoration, Mama called it. The pages were glued on with wood paste and randomly selected: a wall might sport an ad for medicine next to an article on the price of eggs. As the pages yellowed or peeled, Mama slapped fresh ones up. Stella could not remember when she wasn't surrounded by newsprint.

Tonight she reread a piece about what the paper called a crime wave—three robberies—which was next to a story about a college debate team and their success. It seemed like only seconds had passed when she woke with a start as her mother tickled her nose with a feather.

"Thought you weren't sleepy," Mama teased. "You been down for almost two hours! Go get washed—it will be time to leave directly."

Stella sat up, and her mother pulled her close.

"It's gonna be all right," her mother whispered as she smoothed down Stella's hair.

But Stella felt the tension in her mother's arms, and she knew that in reality, fear hugged them both.

"Golly, the outhouse sure is cold this mornin'!" Jojo cried out as he burst in through the front door.

"Well, don't bring the cold in here with you, boy," Mama cried out, releasing Stella. "Shut that door!"

"Yes'm," Jojo said, slamming it behind him as he hurried to the fireplace.

"Stella," Mama said. "Remember to feed the chickens. And see if we got some eggs. Get a move on now."

Stella opened her mouth to complain, to ask why Jojo couldn't help, but a dagger glance from her mother shut her up real quick. She gave the pump handle a few quick jerks, hurriedly splashed water on her face, then headed over to the barn, grabbing the feed sack that hung on the fence as she went. In it was some barley, a little sand for grit, bread crumbs, cornmeal, diced apple peels, and sometimes even bugs or worms. The chickens were always eager for whatever Stella tossed—worms and all. Actually, she thought they were pretty rude, pushing one another out of the way to grab the best morsels. She found three fresh eggs and hightailed it back to the warmth of the house.

Waiting for her on the table was hot-water corn bread smeared with the apple preserves. Stella grinned—Mama made the best apple preserves! Jojo was slurping a bowl of cornmeal mush. Stella could smell onions simmering in the big dented pot on the stove, supper already in progress.

"I saved the last of the preserves for you," Jojo announced.

"Thanks," Stella replied, surprised at his generosity. She munched on the warm, golden-fried bread. *Nobody* made corn bread as good as Mama.

Papa sipped from a mug of coffee, reading one of his three newspapers. "Gotta know what's goin' on in the world," he always reminded Stella when she'd ask why one paper wasn't enough.

The front page of the *Carolina Times* had a story about a Negro college football coach who'd led his team to victory, and another about unfair treatment of colored workers in Raleigh. Sometimes that paper ran articles about Negroes who were responsible for new inventions or discoveries. Those always made Stella sit up a little taller.

She thought about the masthead of that paper. Its motto was "The Truth Unbridled." Stella liked that. Truth. On horseback. Without a saddle or bridle to hold the animal back.

"Can I see one of the other papers, Papa?" she asked, licking her hands free of jelly, glancing at the *Rutherford County News* and the *Forest City Courier*.

"Sure," her father said, pushing them her way without looking up. "Lots of politics and people this week."

Stella couldn't remember when she'd started liking reading the news, but maybe it was because she lived in such a small speck of a town, and she liked how the newspaper helped her feel like she was part of something bigger. Maybe it was because the words on the walls had always been there. She slid both papers closer, taking in events that had happened all over the country—to white people. Colored people were rarely mentioned in those two newspapers. In a curling, fading copy of the *Forest City Courier* glued on the back wall was an article about the local literary club who discussed "The

Negro in Literature" at one of their meetings. It read, "This is a topic about which the average individual knows very little." Stella shook her head every time her gaze fell on that one.

Now, she pushed the papers away. "Papa?"

"Mmm?" he murmured, still reading.

"You think any of the papers will write about the Klan rally last night?" she asked.

Now he looked up. "Oh Lord, no, child. First of all, it was so late, maybe nobody else even saw it. But even if someone had, the white papers will never admit to it happening, and *our* paper would likely be forced out of business." He gave the page he was holding a shake and added ominously, "Or worse."

"I thought the Negro paper believed in reporting the truth," Stella pressed, frowning.

"They believe more in staying alive—" her mother began.

But her father broke in. "Never be afraid to be honest and stand up for what is right, Stella," he said pointedly. "Just remember to balance your courage with wisdom."

"What do you mean?" she asked.

"Catching the Klan is kinda like nailing jelly to a

tree," he explained. "You work real hard, and what do you have to show for it? It just slips down the bark. You understand what I'm saying?"

"Yes, Papa." She understood, but she wasn't sure she *believed* everything he said.

Mama filled Papa's mug back up. "It's chilly out there, Jonah," she said, deliberately changing the subject, Stella thought. "The children are gonna need shoes soon."

Papa blew on the coffee. "They'll be fine. When I was a kid, I never wore shoes. Made me tough. 'Sides, I've got lots more on my mind today than barefoot children."

Stella saw her mother's eyes narrow, but she switched subjects again. "Jojo, Stella, you two get on out of here. Ain't none of the other younguns got shoes neither, so don't you worry at all about that. If you run to school, you'll stay warm. Just be sure to sit by the stove in the schoolroom when you get there."

Stella looked down at her dirty toenails and rusty-looking feet. Shoes might be nice, but she knew those feet could outrun just about anybody in Bumblebee. Well, anybody but Tony Hawkins. And that was good enough for now.

✦ 5 ✦
Quit that Skylarkin'!

As Stella and Jojo got their jackets and lunch pails, their mother warned, "Y'all be careful, you hear! Those crazy Klan folks are up to something. Until we figure out what, you're to come straight home after school. Stay together, stay out of the woods, and keep to the main road."

"You got that?" Papa added.

Stella and Jojo nodded solemnly and headed out into the nippy, sparkling morning. But as soon as they were off the porch, Jojo cried out, "Race ya!" and he took off.

"To the apple tree in the Winstons' yard!" Stella hollered after him, breaking into a run herself.

"Winner gets to be the boss!" Jojo yelled back.

"Well, get ready to lose then!" Stella ran full-out up the dirt road. Laughing and breathless, she touched the tree just seconds before Jojo did, her lunch bucket clunking against the trunk. "Ha-ha! I'm the queen of the world!" she shouted to the sky.

"I almost beat you! You ain't even princess of Bumblebee," Jojo told her, laughing as well.

"I am queen and you gotta do what I say," Stella declared, folding her arms across her chest.

Just then Johnsteve Winston came out of his house, lunch pail dangling from his left hand. He was thick and sturdy, built like a man already.

"She think she's the queen again?" Johnsteve asked Jojo, his thumb pointing to Stella.

"Yup."

Stella fixed them both with a steely glare, then said in her best royal voice, "Both of you must go and slay a dragon for me. Begone!"

Johnsteve raised an eyebrow. "First of all, Your Highness, I didn't lose no race. Second of all, you're in *my* yard."

"And third," Jojo finished, stretching out his arms, "there ain't no dragons around here!"

"Well, how about a bear, then?" Stella asked, hands on her hips.

"Maybe a bear," Johnsteve mused. "But if I caught one, what would you do with it?"

"I'd put it on a leash and take it to church!" Stella said.

"Your sister's crazy," Johnsteve said to Jojo.

"Yup."

Mrs. Winston poked her head out her front door. "Y'all quit that skylarkin' and get your butts to school 'fore you be late! And mind you keep your eyes and ears sharp!"

"Yes, M'am," they all replied, and commenced walking again. The town square, and beyond that, their school, were a little more than a mile away.

"So what all went on at the meeting at your house last night?" Johnsteve asked, changing the mood.

"Far as I can tell, all they did was swear to help and protect each other—and us," Stella said. "I guess it's good they all got together like that, but . . ." She gave a rock a good, hard kick.

"You musta been pretty scared—seeing real live Klansmen!"

"A little," Stella admitted. "Nighttime made them even scarier. But the way I figure it, those robes they wear must look pretty stupid in the daytime."

Randy Bates ambled out of the next house they reached—a small, gray shack, the one on the road most in need of repair. Next door to Randy's house was the home of Dr. Hawkins and his family, freshly white-washed, with geraniums still in bloom by the porch. Now *that*, Stella thought as she did every morning, was like a house in one of her storybooks from school.

Tony ran out the front door and leaped off the porch, sailing right over the geraniums. He pounded Randy on the shoulder. "You're it!" Then he took off in a blaze of speed, his bare feet churning on the dirt.

Randy and Johnsteve scrambled after him, but they gave up after a minute. Tony Hawkins was just too fast. He circled back around to the group.

"I beat you carrying a lunch pail *and* a book!" he crowed victoriously. Tony had an uncle in Raleigh who sent him a box of books every few months. Stella envied that.

"Aw, I let you win," Johnsteve said, giving him a shove.

"Somebody had to stay back and protect Stella and Jojo," Randy added, shoulder-punching them both.

"I can protect myself, thank you very much!" Stella retorted. But she had to admit, this morning especially, it felt good having others around.

Other classmates joined them as they walked down Riverside Road, a name that made no sense to Stella, because it wasn't even close to the river! While Randy and Johnsteve and Tony continued to push one another back and forth, the others seemed more subdued, the youngest ones looking downright nervous.

But as they rounded a bend, Stella perked up—they were nearly at Carolyn's house. Carolyn Malone was Stella's best friend, and not only that, their birthdays were just three days apart. They shared everything— from Stella's worries about school, to how to win at hopscotch, to Carolyn's sorrow when her baby sister, Wilma, had died three months ago. Carolyn ran to meet them, fresh red ribbons tied crisply at the ends of three long braids. That was the only thing they didn't share. Stella's thick, coarse hair never seemed to want to grow much past her ears. Carolyn hugged Stella and tossed a cat's-eye marble at Jojo, who caught it happily.

"How's your mama?" Stella asked her.

"Better, I guess. She still moves pretty slow. Ever since Wilma . . . well, it's like she's scared to get too happy."

Stella gave Carolyn's hand a squeeze. Mama said there was nothing in the world worse than losing a baby.

Helen, Henrietta, Herbert, Hugh, and Hazel—just five of the thirteen Spencer children—straggled out of the last house on the road, the biggest house in all of Bumblebee. It was a true two-floor house, not just a loft upstairs, but a full set of rooms. The Spencers took turns going to school, the rest staying home to help their parents with chores and crops and the babies. The next day, they all switched.

From an upstairs window, Mrs. Spencer called out the same warning she did every morning, "Y'all be good now, 'fore you get knocked to the back side o' nowhere!" Stella had no idea what that meant, though she thought it was funny. But this morning Mrs. Spencer added, "And be watchful, children. Be watchful."

And it seemed to Stella that at every house they passed, parents—some already in work boots or maid uniforms—poked their heads out of doors or stood on porch stoops, warning them, "Shake a leg, y'all," or "Be careful, now."

At the end of Riverside Road, the group turned left onto Main Street. As if on signal, Stella and her friends slowed, dropping their voices to a whisper, then finally growing silent. They couldn't help, every single day, staring at the perfect-looking brick building with perfect-looking grass in the front. Mountain View School. The school for white children.

In addition to a track team, Mountain View had a football team and was known around the state for its academic and sports successes. They even had their own library.

Each morning, as they headed to *their* school, the Mountain View students, most wearing leather shoes and woolen coats against the wind, would sometimes give them a wave as they passed by, sometimes not. But they all knew one another. In a town this small, it was impossible not to.

As the two groups eyed each other, a whoosh of thin, cool air encircled them all. Stella pulled her jacket closer, buttoning up her resentment.

★6★

Silver-Wrapped Chocolate

"Let's go, y'all," Stella urged them forward. "Mrs. Grayson is gonna have a hissy fit if we're late!" Their school was still half a mile away.

The back-and-forth that occurred nearly every morning rose up yet again.

"I wouldn't want to go there," Johnsteve declared. "Too proper!"

"And they wouldn't want you!" Tony countered. "Too dark!"

"You think they got better teachers?" Johnsteve asked.

"Better than Mrs. Grayson?" Stella asked, with a smirk. "Not a chance."

"I like our school, even though it's old," Jojo said.

"And everybody's got ashy legs and scabby knees just like me!"

"Speak for yourself!" Stella retorted.

With that, they all laughed and hurried on to their next stop—Cathy's Candy Store. Mrs. Cathy Cooper opened early so that the children could buy sweet treats on their way to either school. Her twelve-year-old daughter, Thelma, helped her until it was time for her to go to Mountain View.

As they crowded into the store, Stella waved at Mrs. Cooper. She had to be the nicest white lady in Bumblebee, not just because she sometimes gave them free candy, but because she didn't shoo them to the back door like most of the other store owners in town did. It felt kinda good to walk in the front like everybody else. Stopping by the candy store made every day start off sweet.

Carolyn had a penny, so she bought a bag of red hots.

"Thank you, dear," Mrs. Cooper said. "Tell your mama I said hello." Carolyn promised she would.

Stella poked her friend. "Girl, you know I can't eat those things—they make my tongue go thick," she grumbled.

Carolyn grinned. "Maybe that's why I got them!"

"No fair!"

Because they visited the store so often, Stella felt comfortable enough to say hi to Thelma. "It sure must be nice having a mom who owns a candy store," she said this morning.

Thelma laughed. "I probably get less than any of you—Mommy's pretty strict!" She handed Stella a Bazooka Joe bubble gum when her mother wasn't looking.

Just then a group of five white children walked into the store, also carrying lunch pails and school bags. The room was suddenly quiet.

Stella inhaled sharply, a thought striking her. Had any of their fathers been in that field last night?

"Welcome!" Mrs. Cooper called out cheerfully, breaking the uncomfortable silence. "Looks like we've got a full house this morning. Nothing better than a store full of children!"

The two groups, however, moved around each other like oil and water.

Paulette Packard, the doctor's daughter, pushed herself right up to the case and started choosing. Stella could scarcely take her eyes off Paulette's dress—it was a pale lavender, and clearly store-bought. She wore patent-leather shoes and carried a matching pocketbook.

A pocketbook at school? Stella thought.

While most of the children in the store, both black and white, scraped for pennies in their pockets, Paulette pulled out two crisp dollar bills and bought three large bags of candy. She sure liked Goo Goo Clusters!

So as not to be caught staring, Stella turned from Paulette back to Thelma and got up the nerve to ask her something she'd always wondered about. "How's school?"

What Stella really wanted to know was what the rooms looked like—the books, the desks, even the pictures the Mountain View teachers posted on their walls. She would love to have just a teeny peek inside Thelma's classroom.

But Thelma just shrugged. "Grumpy teachers. Lots of reading and reciting. Basically boring. How about yours?"

Stella couldn't understand how school could ever be boring. "It's not bad," was all she told Thelma. But she wondered if white kids ever had trouble figuring out writing and reading stuff.

Barbara Osterman, the daughter of the mill owner, must have been listening, because she stepped close and said in a low voice, "I don't get why we gotta go to different schools anyway. Seems kinda stupid to me."

Stella agreed 100 percent, but she wasn't sure if she was allowed to say that to a white child. She glanced down to pick at the bubble-gum wrapper in her hand.

A tall, thin white boy whom Stella knew only as Kenneth leaned over and whispered to Thelma, "School together? Ha! We don't go to school with them because we don't have to." Stella kept her eyes on the Bazooka as Kenneth went on. "They'll never amount to anything. My daddy says if they learn to cook and sew and clean, that's all they'll need. Hey, can I have some of them Zagnuts?"

Stella wanted to call *him* a Zagnut, or a Dum Dum, or a word that was not a candy, but a curse. Instead she gritted her teeth and looked away to notice that Paulette was slipping out the door. Without her classmates. For a moment Stella wondered if Paulette was uncomfortable with what Kenneth was saying, but she quickly realized that wasn't it. Through the front window she saw Paulette's father on his sleek black stallion, reining in the horse. Paulette hurried to greet him. She held her hand out, and her father smiled and placed a bill in it.

Randy, who'd joined Stella by the window, grabbed her elbow. "Did you see that?" he exclaimed as Paulette tucked the money into her purse and headed across the street to her school. Her father rode off in the other direction, breaking into a full gallop.

"Five dollars!" Stella breathed. "I've never had that much money in my life." But her mind was churning. Dr. Packard's saddle was shiny black. And it was decorated with silver studs that glinted in the sunlight, that would have glimmered in the moonlight. . . .

"All right, young ones," Mrs. Cooper called out, interrupting her thoughts. "I don't want the teachers getting angry at me because you were late for school again. You may each take one Hershey's Kiss as you leave."

As the children from Riverside School and the

children from Mountain View School filed out of the store, each grabbing one silver-wrapped chocolate from Mrs. Cooper's basket, it struck Stella that everyone got the same thing, no matter which school they went to.

★ 7 ★
Piano Frogs

Mrs. Grayson, as they had predicted, was in the doorway waiting for them as they arrived. They were late.

"Is she mad?" Hugh asked, ducking behind his brother.

"Not enough to use the paddle, I don't think," Herbert replied.

Stella thought she saw a hint of a smile cross the teacher's lips as they scooted past her to their desks. Grades one to eleven, about thirty-five students altogether, sat in one room. There was no twelfth grade—students got a diploma and could go to college when they finished eleventh. Stella remembered how proud folks had been last year when Liza Twitty had left for college in Atlanta.

The potbellied stove was already stoked with logs the older students chopped each afternoon. The wooden desks of the younger children sat closest to it, but the whole room felt toasty.

Stella slipped into her own seat, next to the upright piano that Mrs. Grayson plinked out hymns and folk songs and ballads on. The thing was ancient, but Mrs. Grayson managed to work around the keys that were out of tune.

In the front of the room stood the American flag, which always tilted a little to the right in its stand. On the front wall were silhouettes of George Washington and Abraham Lincoln, a map of the world, and a map of North Carolina. A red thumbtack marked the location of Bumblebee, smack-dab between Spindale and Forest City.

After the Pledge of Allegiance and morning prayer, Mrs. Grayson announced that they had a great deal to do that day, including arithmetic for all grades.

Everyone groaned.

The teacher held up a hand. "But first we have something to discuss." Once she had everyone's attention, she said, "I know you've all heard about what was seen in the woods last night. And I know your parents have warned you all to be careful. Let me add my two cents. Don't *ever* walk alone—stay in groups. Do not go into the woods for any reason. If you see anything that looks out of place, run—I say *run*—and find an adult. I am always here for you, and you are safe when you're with me. Any questions?"

Jojo was the first to raise his hand. "The—those—they—they wouldn't hurt children . . . would they?"

Mrs. Grayson looked Jojo in the eye. "Let's just not take any chances. Is that clear? Now, for something far more jolly, how about we start the day by practicing for the Christmas pageant!"

While her classmates began murmuring happily, Stella couldn't shake a sudden feeling of foreboding. Christmas was still a good ten weeks off. Why were they starting so early? Then it dawned on her that Mrs. Grayson was trying to distract them. It sure worked with Jojo.

"Ooh, when is it? Where's it gonna be?" her brother asked, not bothering to raise his hand this time.

"Jojo, where you been? At New Hope Church, as always!" the teacher replied. "Christmas Eve, just like we've been doing forever. It's our Christmas gift to Bumblebee—to our parents and friends and everybody in our community. Why, I remember you weren't even walking yet when you first played Baby Jesus."

Jojo beamed.

"We all get parts?" Carolyn asked, glancing at Stella excitedly.

"Of course. Every one of you has a part—"

Randy broke in, "Even *all* the Spencers?"

Everyone laughed, and Mrs. Grayson smiled. "Yes, the whole Spencer clan. All thirteen of them. Even little Hetty! Now, I'm going to expect you older students to help the young ones, and please tell your folks I'll need some bedsheets and feed sacks for costumes."

"And cookies!" Herbert reminded her.

"And candy!" Jojo added.

"Yes, yes, yes, of course, but let's start with memorizing our lines before we plan the menu," Mrs. Grayson said, holding her hands up.

"What's more important than dessert?" Johnsteve asked.

"Some might say music," she replied. "I want to start with one of the songs we'll sing that night. A new one. And"—she gave a sly smile—"we'll do some arithmetic at the same time!"

Math and music? Stella looked to Carolyn, who made a *don't ask me* face.

Mrs. Grayson walked over to the piano and started lifting the lid. Before it was even all the way up, she let out a screech. Everyone jumped up. "I do declare!" Mrs. Grayson exclaimed, staggering backward as two fat frogs leaped from the piano. "Good gracious, my Lord!"

Henrietta, whose desk, like Stella's, was close to the piano, leaped away screaming. Johnsteve and Hugh and Carolyn were already on the floor, scrambling under seats, trying to catch the frogs. Randy had both hands up high in the air, yelling, "It wasn't me!" Everyone else looked about ready to pop with held-in giggles, but the look on Mrs. Grayson's face was a thunderstorm.

"Which of you boys did this?" she demanded. "Johnsteve? Tony?"

Tony shook his head, sputtering, "We didn't do it. Honest."

"You Spencer boys?"

Herbert held one of the squirming, leggy frogs in one hand. Hugh held the other. Their eyes were wide with innocence. Herbert spoke up first. "We didn't bring no frogs in here, miss. But can we keep 'em?"

That stopped Mrs. Grayson short. "Keep them? For pets?"

"No, M'am," Hugh answered. "For to eat. My sister Hannah can put 'em in some stew!"

Mrs. Grayson's eyes finally softened. Herbert was awfully thin and hungry-looking. Stella hoped Mrs. Grayson would say yes.

"Do what you want with them, boys. Put them in those old Mason jars over there, poke a few holes in the top. Mind now that they don't get loose again."

As Herbert and Hugh hurried off, Mrs. Grayson turned to the rest of the class. "I still need to know which young man hid frogs in my piano! Jojo, was it you?"

"No, M'am. I promise," Jojo replied. "But you gotta admit—it *was* kinda funny."

Mrs. Grayson did not look amused.

Stella looked around, as curious as her teacher. Finally one small hand went into the air.

"It was me, Mrs. Grayson," Claudia Odom said quietly.

Mrs. Grayson didn't seem quite sure how to respond. She'd clearly been prepared to swat a naughty boy, and now looked at the first grader in astonishment. As did Stella. "Claudia? But . . . why?"

"I like stuff like frogs and snakes and bugs," Claudia said simply. "I found them last night, and I put them in my lunch pail to show everybody."

"So . . . how did they end up in my piano?" The teacher looked flabbergasted.

"I figured they needed some exercise. I was gonna move them at lunch. You don't ever do music until afternoon. I didn't mean to scare you."

"I most certainly was not frightened," Mrs. Grayson said, straightening her back. "Just very surprised." She pursed her lips tightly, tried to look angry, then finally, explosively, she burst out with the biggest laugh Stella had ever heard from her. "Lord have mercy, child!" she cried out. "Don't ever do that to me again! That's about all the botheration a body can stand for one day!"

"Can I still keep 'em?" Hugh called out from where he was jabbing holes into a Mason jar lid.

"Sure, Hugh," Claudia said amiably. "Kilkenny Pond is full of frogs!"

Stella found herself thinking about the frogs she'd heard in the pond. What might a family of bullfrogs have witnessed under the darkness of other nights?

★8★
Go Where I Send Thee

"Well, we have wasted quite enough time with frogs and foolishness," Mrs. Grayson said, buttoning up her smiles. "So let's get started. Most of you probably have heard this song, but we need to make sure we have the words and rhythms right. This is for a performance." She raised an eyebrow at Claudia. "I trust no other animals shall land in my lap while we proceed?" Then she sat down at the old piano, and her fingers seemed to glide over the keys.

Stella grinned as she recognized the tune. She'd learned it when she was only two or three, sitting on her granny's lap at church. She suddenly remembered sliding the thin band of silver—her grandmother's wedding ring—up and down her granny's thin fingers.

Now Mrs. Grayson, pulling the children into the heart of the song, began to sing. "First verse!" she called out.

"Children, go where I send thee
How shall I send thee?
I'm gonna send thee one by one
One was the little bitty baby
Born in Bethlehem."

"I know this one," Jojo cried. "It gets longer and longer."

"And faster and faster!" Henrietta added.

"You should be singing, not talking," Mrs. Grayson told them, keeping to the song's melody as she did so.

"Verse two," Mrs. Grayson now called out. "As you can see, we are doing our arithmetic lessons while we sing!"

"Children, go where I send thee
How shall I send thee?
I'm gonna send thee two by two

Two was Paul and Silas
One was the little bitty baby
Born in Bethlehem."

The teacher kept adding more verses until they had completed all twelve:

"Children, go where I send thee
How shall I send thee?
I'm gonna send thee twelve by twelve
Twelve was the twelve that couldn't get help
Eleven was the 'leven that all went to heaven
Ten was the Joseph brothers
Nine was the nine all dressed so fine
Eight was the eight who stood at the gate
Seven was the seven couldn't get to heaven
Six was the six that never got picked
Five was the five that came back alive
Four was the four that stood at the door
Three was the three old wise men
Two was Paul and Silas
One was the little bitty baby
Born in Bethlehem."

"Wonderful!" Mrs. Grayson said. "Let's do it again, but faster this time!" And so they did. Over and over, faster and faster, until they were all breathless with laughter and song.

Then Mrs. Grayson abruptly stopped playing. "I know it's not in the song, but how much is three *times* three?" she demanded.

"Nine!" Johnsteve responded quickly.

She nodded with approval, then looked at the students in the lower grades. "How much is three *plus* three?"

"Six!" Jojo chirped.

"She sure did figure out a way to do it!" Carolyn whispered to Stella.

To the older children she said, "Four times four?"

"Sixteen!"

"Twelve times twelve?"

"One hundred and forty four! Too easy," Tony said.

"Excellent!" The teacher looked pleased. "Now, children," she continued cheerfully, "let's begin our writing projects. I will collect them at the end of the day."

Stella slumped in her seat. Writing. The perfect way to ruin a perfect morning.

Mrs. Grayson divided everyone into groups by grades. She tasked the oldest students with looking up each reference from the song in the Bible and figuring out who were the "eight who stood at the gate," then writing about one of them. The little ones were told to write short word stories or poems about Christmas.

When Mrs. Grayson got to Stella's group of nine- to twelve-year-olds, she told them, "I want each of you to write an essay—an opinion piece. It should be one to two pages in length. Your best penmanship."

Two pages? Stella's stomach curled into knots.

Mrs. Grayson caught Stella's eye. "Just write down what you think about what happened last night," she suggested. "Bumblebee belongs to all of us, and what happens here is important."

Outside the classroom window stood an ancient apple tree, its branches gnarled and entwined. They'd all feasted on the fruit since the start of school, but the last of the apples had fallen in the past week. Stella gazed out at the few remaining leaves stirring in the sharp breeze. When she opened her notebook, her thoughts snarled like those tangled branches. Stella didn't like to write.

When she was in first grade, she had been the worst reader in the whole class. It had taken her longer than anyone else to figure out the connection between words in her head and the charts of both printed and cursive versions of the ABCs on the wall. Reading and writing had come slowly to Stella, in spite of her mother's wallpaper. Mrs. Grayson, so patient, had let Stella work at her own pace, but still she'd struggled with putting it all together. Even now, for sure, she'd never be the class spelling bee champion like Carolyn.

So instead of beginning her essay, Stella busied herself with getting ready to get ready. She had a system—pencils on the left, notebook on the right, books in the middle. She liked everything neat and lined up so the edges matched.

Not that any of that mattered, she thought glumly. A neat desk couldn't disguise the inside of her notebook, which was a jumble of half-finished work, scratch-outs, and mess-ups. Arithmetic wasn't so bad—numbers lined up in an order that made sense to her. But writing, oh Lordy.

It wasn't that she didn't have strong opinions on lots of things. She sure did! But putting them on paper just wasn't her piece of cake. Or pie. Or pancakes with molasses, which she dearly loved. Writing was more like trying to chew an unripe apple—bitter and hard and not worth the effort. Worse—she even had a couple of bad grades in that notebook that she'd hidden from her parents, which she knew was dumb. Eventually her mama and Mrs. Grayson would get to talking at church, and her life would be over.

And it wasn't that her mind wasn't spinning with ideas—images of flames, of those stamping horses, wore sharp in her memory. It was getting them straight in her notebook. . . .

Mrs. Grayson gave her a questioning look, clearly noting Stella had yet to put one word to paper. So Stella finally picked up a pencil. She scratched out words. Started again. Erased half of it with her almost-nub-like gum eraser. Started again. Stopped.

Shoulders slumped, she stared back out the window. A breeze blew a few curled and ruddy leaves from the apple tree. Stella figured sticking those leaves back on the branches would be easier than trying to move the stuff in her head to the empty blue lines in her notebook.

★ 9 ★
Wise Men

I have ~~not~~ no idea where ~~bethlaham~~
Bethelehem is. I guess the wise men must
of been pretty wise to find it.

When the baby Jesus was born, there
was a ~~brite~~ bright light in the sky. It was
a good star, the ~~preshure~~ preacher says.
The kings and the wise men ~~follewd foulled~~
chased it.

Last night me and Jojo saw a fire that
lit up the dark. It was a not good very bad
sign. Scary. No ~~angles~~ angels showed up in
the sky, and nobody sang any pretty carols.

The only wise men I saw were in my
mama's kitchen.

Stella could think of nothing more to say. She frowned. She started to raise her hand to ask for help, but Mrs. Grayson was busy with the third graders, who seemed to be having no trouble at all with their writing projects.

Dunce! She ripped the page out of her notebook, balled it up, and put her head down on her desk.

When Mrs. Grayson stopped by to check on Stella with a gentle hand on her shoulder, Stella mumbled something about a stomachache, and the teacher left her alone the rest of the afternoon.

Stella never finished her assignment.

✦ 10 ✦
Treasures in a Cigar Box

"I must give this paper an F, Stella," Mrs. Grayson told Stella sadly at the end of the day, catching her as she was walking out the schoolhouse door. "It's incomplete. It's got potential, but you gave up. Perhaps I should stop by your house with a plate of gingersnaps and have a chat with your mama."

"Oh, please don't do that," Stella begged in alarm. "I'll finish it tonight and bring it in tomorrow. I promise."

"I know the writing part can be a challenge for you, Stella," Mrs. Grayson said. "You read well. You think well. All you need to do is make the leap to putting it down on paper. And actually, the little that you wrote here is pretty good. But," she added sternly, "you can do better."

Wishing a hole big enough to swallow her would appear in the floor, Stella couldn't look at the teacher. "Yes, M'am," she mumbled.

"Try this, Stella." Mrs. Grayson pulled her pocketbook from the bottom desk drawer. "Write about *yourself*. You are the expert on you. I shall expect a finished paper in the morning, or I may be joining ya'll for supper tomorrow. Understood? Now get on home before your mama starts to wondering why Jojo got there first."

Stella nodded, thanked the teacher, then hurried down the road. And thankfully, her mother was busy with the vegetable garden, so she didn't notice Stella slipping in a little later than usual.

Stella raced through her chores, making sure the carrots were sliced perfectly, the potatoes peeled thinly, and the table cleaned and shined for dinner. She felt jumpy—anxious for the night, hopeful that no fiery disturbances would mar the darkness this time, and worried that her mother would find out she'd gotten in trouble at school.

Hours later, after dinner, after Jojo's good-night book, Stella was still worried—it was taking everyone far too long to fall asleep! Stella waited and waited.

The blaze in the fireplace had died down to embers, only whispers and ashen shadows remaining of the roaring fire of a few hours ago. Jojo lay on his cot close to the hearth, with Dusty curled beside him. At last, Father started snoring loudly with gasps and grunts between—when Stella teased him about it each morning, however, he'd swear that he never made a noise.

And finally, slowly, ever so slowly, Stella tiptoed across the floor, carefully avoiding the floorboard that she knew would creak. Nobody stirred. The dog raised his head briefly but went back to sleep.

Stella grabbed Papa's work jacket from the nail by the door. The door itself did not squeak when she opened it. She'd thought ahead—after dinner she had oiled the hinge with a dab of lard. Now she smiled as she pressed the door shut and inhaled the crispness of the night air. But still wary, she stood still. She listened. Silence. She waited. Nothing.

The night sky was an inky blue-black blanket strewn with thousands of crystal-bright stars. A half-moon added even more light. When she was satisfied that all was well, she sat on the second step and reached under the third, searching deeper and deeper until her fingers found what she was searching for. She pulled out the school notebook that she'd stuffed under there after school, as well as a package wrapped in a piece of worn leather. Inhaling the rich animal smell of it, she unwrapped it slowly. There lay Stella's treasure—an old cigar box.

She lifted the lid, the scent of tobacco wafting out, and sifted through the items inside—dozens of yellowing and curled newspaper articles she'd torn from Papa's discarded newspapers, from news stories not pasted on the wall. She'd started collecting them after a school assignment last year.

- There was one about a lady named Amelia Earhart. She flies all by herself in a small plane across the ocean.

- Another one about two men named Laurel and Hardy, who are famous for being a funny comedy team.

- And more: Amos and Andy are famous for being funny also, but they are played by

white men who pretend to be Negro. The
colored newspaper explains this part.

- A man named Hitler from Germany has
  lots of soldiers following him. He calls them
  storm troopers.

- Someone kidnaps the baby of a man named
  Charles Lindbergh. The baby dies.

- Lots of people have no jobs because of something called the Depression. A man named
  Roosevelt promises to fix that if he is elected
  president.

Stella also collected local stories.

- Miss Erma Thorndike wins first place in the
  Miss Corn Cob contest.

- Clifford Eubanks gets arrested for being
  drunk on a Sunday.

o Dinah Lee Dixon grows the biggest pumpkin
    in the county—it weighs thirty-three pounds,
    seven ounces.

The world, she had found, was so much bigger than Bumblebee. And so much more exciting.

Stella set the clippings aside and began flipping through a couple of pages of the notebook from school, frowning. She just couldn't seem to get it right, this writing thing. She did most of her homework with Jojo at the kitchen table. But she practiced her writing at night—she didn't want her family to know how she messed up. Mama and Papa, of course, expected her to bring home good grades in every subject. Ugh.

Finally Stella opened the notebook to a fresh page. Taking an idea from her father's newspaper that morning, she wrote just one word on that page—*TRUTH*. The whole rest of the page was an ocean of white. Double ugh. She chewed on the pencil. She made curlicues on each letter of *TRUTH*. Then she made a decision. If she was gonna really write with honesty, she ought to start, like Mrs. Grayson said, with herself.

She gripped the pencil so tight, it made a mark on her middle finger.

It took five tries to get it right. Five balled-up sheets of paper. Five pages of anger and mess-ups and erasures. When she finished, she rubbed her eyes, sleep begging to creep in.

She read it over one last time, not really satisfied, but it was the truth. Even if it still had some scratch-outs.

★ 11 ★
TRUTH

~~My name is Stella and I am me.~~

~~My name is Estelle and I am somebody.~~

My name is Estelle Mills, and I am not nobody. Mrs. Grayson would say that's a ~~dubble~~ double negative. Well, I'm here to say I'm not no negative. I am me, and that's a fact.

I like to be called Stella because it reminds me of stars, and I like the night. Mama tells me I was born at ~~midnite~~ midnight during a full moon. Maybe that is why.

I am left-handed—the only student in the whole school who is.

My family reminds me of good things to drink.

Mama is hot chocolate.

Papa is black coffee.

Jojo is sweet tea.

Me, I'm the color of rum. Mama cooks with it sometimes.

I've got thick black hair, and bushy caterpillar-looking eyebrows. When I look in the mirror, I don't see pretty. I just see me.

Besides, sometimes things that look pretty, like secret fire in the darkness, are really pretty ugly.

⋆ 12 ⋆
Spoon Man's Coming!

Saturday morning bloomed bright like, hmm, Stella tried to think of a description her teacher would like. *A sky full of daylilies! That wasn't so bad,* Stella thought. She had turned the paper in to Mrs. Grayson yesterday, who had grunted with approval and given her a grade of C. Stella, relieved, wondered if there would still be a conversation between her teacher and her mother. Mrs. Grayson did not say, and Stella for sure didn't ask.

So that afternoon, when Mama told Stella to get Papa's hammer and a few nails and fix some porch planks that had worked loose, she'd jumped at the chance to be helpful, just in case. "Ouch!" she cried out, putting her thumb in her mouth for the second time that day. Holding the nail was easy. Banging it into the wood was a little trickier.

Bap! Bap! Bap! She finally had a rhythm going, enjoying the sun on her back, when Jojo looked up from slapping whitewash on the front fence. "Lookie, Stella!" he cried out all of a sudden, happily. "Spoon Man's coming!"

Stella dropped the hammer, swung open the front door, and hollered, "Hey, Mama! The Spoon Man— he's coming up the road, Mama! Come outside quick!"

Her mother rushed out to the porch, a bandanna on her head, a scrub brush in her hand, and a grudging smile on her face. "Well-a, well-a. Lordy be."

"Can we look? Please, Mama? Can we look at what he's got?"

"Of course, honeygirl." Her mother dried her hands on her apron. "I might even take a gander at his goods myself." Jojo and Stella raced ahead of her.

"What you bring me, Spoon Man?" Jojo demanded, meeting the visitor before he even pulled into the yard. "You got candy?" Dusty sniffed suspiciously at the mule pulling the wagon.

Spoon Man, whose real name was Terence

Oglethorpe, was a large, almond-brown man, almost as wide as the wagon itself, his belly ballooning over his belt. His shirt, made of what might have been a feed sack, was covered by a huge yellow vest decorated with red tulips. His trousers sported multiple patches of various colors and materials, and his purple velveteen jacket had buttons made from—were those spools of thread? When he greeted them with a tip of his straw hat with the shimmering blue feather, his huge smile revealed only occasional teeth. Stella could only gape.

Spoon Man traveled all over North Carolina, plying curios and cookware, tools and trinkets—and news. Thirsty for information about friends and family and folks from all around, everyone loved Spoon Man's visits—sometimes he even carried mail and packages, saving folks the cost of stamps.

Climbing down ponderously from the wooden buckboard, he tossed Stella and Jojo each a piece of molasses taffy.

"Where you been, Spoon Man?" Stella asked, unwrapping the candy. "I'd give anything to travel round like you do. I bet you have all kinds of adventures."

Spoon Man leaned back and stretched. "If you

think bumping my backside on this hard seat all day long is an adventure, you better rethink, girl."

Stella barely heard him—she'd already moved to the rear of his wagon, standing on tippy-toes to better eye the treasures that he kept back there.

"Tell your mama I got a purty little bracelet made of purple glass that I been savin' just for you, Stella," Spoon Man called out. "Only ten cents."

Stella whirled around to her mother, who'd just caught up. "Can I, Mama? Can I have it, please? Oh please, Mama. I'll do all my chores for a month without complaining even once."

"You'll do that anyway," her mother replied wryly. She turned to Spoon Man. "How you doin', Mr. Oglethorpe? It's been a couple of months since you made it to these parts."

"Oh, I be fine, Miz Mills. Been here and there and everywhere. And I got forty-leven things to show you!"

"That many, you say?"

He made a clumsy bow, hat in hand. "Yours is the first house in Bumblebee that I have the honor to stop at. I brung you some fabric, a bit of thread, a new set of spoons, and a full set of fixin' tools for your husband."

"Now, you know money's tight, Mr. Oglethorpe," Mama said, tapping her foot, putting on her stern face.

"You ain't alone, M'am. Times is rough all around. This here Depression is downright depressin'!" He gave a hoot and slapped his thigh at his own joke.

Mama looked him up and down. Despite his wide girth, his cheeks looked hollow. "You hungry?" she asked.

"I ain't had a good meal since I left Raleigh," Spoon Man admitted. "Even my mule is saggin'."

"I tell you what," Mama said. "I'll send the children round to the neighbors. If everybody brings a little bit of food, why, we'll all have a great supper, you can tell us about your travels, and you might could even sell a couple trinkets while you're at it."

"Well, thank you, M'am!" Spoon Man said, tipping his hat to her again. "I'd be mighty obliged."

"Stella, Jojo, run go tell everybody to bring a little potluck if they can. Tell 'em to bring the younguns, bring the old folks. We gonna have stories and feastin' tonight! Lordy! It's what we all need right now."

Stella and Jojo didn't have to be told twice. They darted down the road, and by the time they got back, the mule had been fed and tied to a tree near the barn, Spoon Man was sitting on their front porch, and, by the magnolia, Dr. Hawkins was helping Papa lay planks of wood across four tree stumps. Mama threw a bedsheet over the whole thing, and like magic, it had become a supper table! Then Papa added logs to the fire pit, readying it for a toasty blaze.

Spoon Man, Stella noticed, simply sat there and watched the activity around him, sipping from a cup of sweet tea, nibbling Mama's sugar cookies, and burping occasionally. The man was a burper, that was for sure. But Stella knew his turn was coming—he was saving his energy for the storytelling. Nobody in town could hold a candle to the Spoon Man when it came to unfolding a tale.

Neighbors started arriving, armed with logs for the fire pit as well as food. "Jojo, run get some kindlin' from the woodpile and stack it here," Papa told him. "And be mindful of snakes, boy. They like to sleep up under them logs. You wake 'em up, they ain't gonna be happy!"

Jojo, with Dusty at his heels, was back in a blink with a handful of twigs.

Papa took them, saying, "More, boy. We need lots. Bigger pieces. Take your time," and sent Jojo off again. He took a seat beside Spoon Man. Jojo and the dog disappeared once more.

How much kindling did Papa need? Stella wondered. *Ah!* She figured it out—Papa was keeping Jojo out of everyone's way for a little while, because he was fixing to say something to Spoon Man he didn't want Jojo to hear. She quietly lowered herself to the middle step and pretended to pick a splinter from the bottom of her foot.

Spoon Man wasted no time getting to the point. "So, I hear tell y'all got some Klan worries here in Bumblebee."

Stella's father's eyebrows arched. "I reckon that kind of news travels fast."

Spoon Man leaned forward. "Even a one-legged rumor gets around after a while," he said with a chuckle. "And this one was wearin' speed skates!"

"What you been hearin'?" Stella's father asked.

Stella watched out of the corner of her eye as Spoon Man chomped down on his third cookie and covered his mouth to stifle another burp. "Well, everywhere I go, folks is hungry. Crops failin.' Cows comin' up dry. Bosses ain't payin'. The way I see it, people be lookin' for change, for something to believe in."

Dr. Hawkins came up and poured himself some tea from the enamel pitcher Mama had placed on a fruit crate, then joined Papa and Spoon Man. "Well, we all know about the election comin' up next month," he said. "Everybody says Franklin Delano Roosevelt is gonna be in the White House."

"Folks sick of Hoover—that's for sure," Spoon Man said.

"I sure would like to cast my vote," Papa added.

Stella sat ramrod straight. What?

"Now, you know they don't want us to votin'," Spoon Man chided, tipping his chair back on two legs. "Maybe that's why they all of a sudden wearin' the bedsheets off their clotheslines again."

"Look, I'm not lookin' for trouble. I just think I ought to be able to vote," her father said evenly.

"What for?" Mr. Bates asked, coming up to the porch, taking his time as he climbed with his crutch. He'd contracted polio a few years back—the only person in town who had, as far as Stella knew. She scooted to the far side of the steps to give him room and began rubbing each of her toenails clean with a little bit of spit, hoping she'd stay unnoticed.

"Won't make no difference nohow. Won't put a nickel in your pocket or a biscuit on your table," Spoon Man argued reasonably.

"It would to me," her father replied stubbornly. "I live in this country and I ain't no slave, and dagummit, I oughta be allowed to vote!"

Dr. Hawkins swirled his tea around and gazed into the bronze liquid. "Jonah, I've looked into this. You know they've gone and set up these poll taxes."

"I know."

"And a literacy test about the Constitution you gotta pass."

Stella's father set his jaw. "I know all that."

"Get ready for questions like, 'How many bubbles in a bar of soap?' or 'How many wrinkles in an elephant's trunk?'" Spoon Man said.

Stella noticed that not one of the men even smiled. This was dead serious.

"And the KKK? They get a report of *any* colored person who tries to register to vote. You want that hammer hangin' over your family?" Mr. Bates's face went angry. "You already got them burning crosses practically in your backyard!"

Her father looked to the distance, out across the pond. "Sometimes I just get tired of bowin' down and givin' up, you know?"

It was Dr. Hawkins who nodded in agreement. He placed a hand on Papa's broad shoulder, but then he added, "You know, Jonah, sometimes it's best to wait till times get better."

"And when will that be?"

Stella hunkered over her toes. She knew none of them had an answer.

13
Sweet Potato Pie and Fried Green Tomatoes

Jojo came staggering back, this time with a pile of kindling higher than his head. Stella hopped up to help him.

"Anything else you need me to do?" she asked her father once she'd piled the kindling by the logs.

"Go see if you can help your mother. Don't know what made the wife plan this all sudden-like," he grumbled.

In the kitchen Stella hardly knew where to begin— Mama was already a whirlwind of activity. One moment she was bent over a boiling kettle, then turning meat in a sizzling pan, then hovering by the table as she baked, battered, and tossed several different foods, seemingly all at once. With flushed cheeks and sweaty face, she at last looked up and grinned. "I'm lovin' this, you know," she told Stella, pausing to take a sip of lemonade.

Stella admitted to her mother what she'd been thinking as she'd watched her. "How can you do that all at once? I will *never* be able to do what you do."

"I felt the same way at your age, Stella. My mother had seven children—I don't think she had a good night's sleep in twenty years," Mama joked, reaching over to flip a slice of spitting bacon. "I still don't know how she did it."

Well, that wasn't a helpful answer, Stella thought. Her mother must have sensed it, for she added, "Don't worry, honeygirl. Things fall into place when they should."

Well, that wasn't helpful either!

"Tonight I might be plum wore out, but today the sun is shining, we got company, and life is good!" her mother continued cheerfully. Then she spun around to check on the biscuits in the oven.

"Can I help?" Stella said, taking the stirring spoon from her and peeping into the pot. "What are we makin'?"

"Killed lettuce. Quick, easy, and—" Mama paused and wiped her forehead.

"And yummy," Stella finished for her. The bacon fat was crackling, along with red onions and slabs of garden potatoes. Ohhh, it smelled so fine. As Mama tossed the lettuce in, the green leaves wilted immediately, absorbing the liquid and the flavor.

Carolyn lunged through the front door, toting a large pan. "My mama sent pinto beans," she announced, placing it on the table. "That woulda been all we had for supper tonight, but now we get a feast!"

"Tell your mama her beans will go perfect with the killed lettuce. I hope Mrs. Odom is bringin' her famous corn pone," Stella's mother said as she stirred another pot.

Just then two of the Spencer girls knocked on the front door. "We brought collard greens and fried green tomatoes, Mrs. Mills," Hannah said.

Stella whispered to Carolyn, "Glad she didn't send frog legs!"

"Just set everything on the big table outside, girls, and thank you kindly," Stella's mother sang out. "And Stella," she added, "go find Tony and Johnsteve and Randy, and ask them to bring over some chairs, would you?"

"Yes, Mama." Stella ran out to find the boys, who were already sneaking samples of okra and hush puppies from the makeshift table. Without even thinking, she popped Tony's hand as he was about to swipe a fingerful of icing from a cake. He looked at her with a smirk. "My mama said get some chairs so we can eat," Stella said, a flush coming to her cheeks. The boys swiped one more hush puppy each and trotted back toward their houses.

The makeshift table was soon overflowing with food—oatmeal cookies, cheese grits, hot biscuits and honey, a sweet potato pie, Apple Brown Betty, black-eyed peas, fried chicken, corn pudding, pulled pork, and pickled pigs' feet. Every single family brought just a little something. Pastor Patton and his wife from New Hope Church brought a pot of chicken and dumplings.

Mrs. Grayson arrived carrying a carrot cake. She nodded toward all the food, then winked at Stella. *Oh, thank you! Thank you! Thank you!* Stella knew there would be no discussion of school problems this evening.

She began carting out her mama's food, but once

the boys were back, they plunked the chairs down and organized a massive game of capture the flag. The children chased one another until everyone was panting, the perfect moment for her to zero in on Johnsteve, who had the flag in hand—a rag from Mama's sewing basket—and grab it from him.

"I am the champion!" Stella cried as she shimmied away from Helen and Henrietta, who were trying to snatch the flag from her, only to have Tony swing back around and swipe it from her at the last moment.

Then Randy let out the cry, "Time to eat, y'all!" The flag was forgotten. Pastor Patton blessed the food, and everyone's attention turned to what ended up being a real feast.

Stella waited to let others go ahead of her before getting in line, as she knew her mother would want. Folks sat anywhere they could—on the ground, on the porch, on the various chairs that the boys had dragged down the road. Spoon Man wove in and out, offering a pair of earrings to Mrs. Bates, and a new hacksaw to Mr. Spencer.

"You sure would look pretty in a new dress," he purred to Claudia's mother, holding up a bolt of butter-yellow linen. "Even got enough here so you can make a dress for little Claudia, too. One dollar for two yards. You can't get this at the general store."

Mrs. Odom frowned and fretted, fingering the soft fabric, but finally pulled out four quarters from a knotted handkerchief.

After most folks had been served, Stella picked up a plate, relieved that the boys had left a few hush puppies—they were one of her favorites too. She took a little extra of her other favorite, the corn pudding. Perching on a wobbly kitchen chair, balancing the plate on her lap, she set into devouring foods seasoned by other mothers' hands—familiar, yet different from what her own mama cooked. Sweet potatoes glazed with sugar. Crisp string beans and onions. Yeast rolls soft as pillows.

All the while, Spoon Man quietly meandered through the crowd, selling a frying pan, a box of buttons, a kerosene lamp, and a fishing pole. Then, oh happiness, she saw her mother give Spoon Man ten pennies for that purple glass bracelet, which Mama then quickly tucked into her apron pocket. It was the only thing she bought.

In between, Spoon Man knocked back two heaping plates of food, plus several kinds of dessert. He finally ambled over to Stella. "So, how's school?" he asked as he sat down heavily beside her.

"Not bad, but not so good sometimes," she said evasively, popping the last of her mother's dumplings into her mouth. "I like arithmetic."

Spoon Man studied her. "School stuff feels kinda pale when you think about what you and Jojo saw. Am I right?"

Instead of answering, Stella concentrated on the last kernels of corn pudding. But she felt Spoon Man's continued gaze and finally admitted that she felt a little scared.

"You got a right to be. You were a witness. That's important."

"I kinda wish I hadn't seen it," Stella told him. "It's like a bad photograph I can't get out of my head!"

"Know what I do when something's stuck in my mind?"

"What?"

"I grab me a scrap of paper and write it down. It be out of my head then, and onto the paper."

Stella narrowed her eyes slightly.

"Hey, you don't think old Spoon Man knows his letters and numbers? Girl, I got more learnin' than you know!"

"Oh, I wasn't thinking that. It's just that, that . . ." She shrugged in defeat. "I'm not so good at writing."

With a hefty *"Oomph,"* Spoon Man stood up. He chucked her under the chin. "Give it a try, Stella. Trust the words. Maybe that image will fade."

Stella shook her head doubtfully. "I'm no story-teller," she told him as she walked away. "I can't do what you do."

★14★
The Chicken Who Was an Eagle

Stella watched Spoon Man wander over toward where the neighbors, like moths, were hovering over the warmth of the fire pit. The odd flame shot up, and while the sight of it sent a flicker of a shiver through Stella, she also noticed that the fire's glow gave everyone a blush of peacefulness. Any threat, for now, seemed distant.

"Ooh-wee, this was a good idea, Georgia," Mrs. Spencer told Stella's mother as she finished her third piece of pie. "I was good and hungry!" She was a tall woman with a huge gap between her two front teeth and the biggest laugh in the neighborhood. Stella had never seen her lose her temper or yell at one of her children, not even once.

"I heard once about a man who was so hungry he salted and peppered himself and swallowed himself whole!" Mr. Bates said, slapping his skinny knee.

"That's nothin'," countered Mr. Winston. "I know a man who was so hungry he ate up his skin and bones and left nothin' but his shadow!"

Loud guffaws followed.

Mr. Spencer jumped in. "Well, I know a man so stingy that he wouldn't eat out in the sunlight, 'cause he was scared his shadow might ask for some of the food!" His wife howled.

Mr. Winston, who worked in the mill with Mr. Spencer, added, "Now *I* know 'bout stingy. The *boss* be stingy. I know a boss so cheap that one day when the mine blowed up and some of the workers got blown in the air, he docked their pay for the time their feet wasn't on the ground."

"Smitherman," several men said at once, nodding. Everybody seemed to be in agreement at that one. An uncomfortable silence suddenly fell.

Stella's father looked over at Spoon Man's mule, and, clearly trying to lighten the mood, quickly called out, "Your mule sho is skinny, Spoon Man. But I know a man whose mule was so thin that he had to feed that animal muddy water just to keep from seeing through it!" That brought the laughter back.

Mrs. Malone, sipping from a mug, said, "Sarah Bates, this is some right good cider. You ever heard tell of the man who grew an apple so big that when it fell in the river one day, the river ran pure cider for six months?"

"No," Mrs. Bates replied. "But I know 'bout an apple tree that grew so tall that it took fifty years to cut it down. My great uncle started sawing it in 1882, and it just fell yesterday!"

Stella cracked up—that was a good one!

Dr. Hawkins stretched his hands out toward the fire pit. "Winter comin' soon. I remember that day it got so cold that my words got frozen as they come out my mouth. I had to take 'em inside by the fire and melt 'em before my family knew what I was saying!"

Mr. Spencer added, "Yeah, but remember last summer when it got so hot we had to feed the chickens ice water to keep them from laying hard-boiled eggs?"

The laughter rippled across the darkness like a silken ribbon.

"Well, what about that storm that blew the crooked road straight?"

"The same wind that blowed so hard the sun came up late and Sunday didn't get here until late Tuesday evening?" Pastor Patton joined in.

"That's musta been why I missed church last week," Mr. Winston said.

"You missed church because you went fishing!" Pastor Patton retorted.

Mr. Winston turned to Spoon Man. "Save me, Spoon Man," he pleaded. "Tell us a story before the pastor sends me to damnation for a fishin' trip!"

"Can't help you much there, John," Spoon Man replied with a smile. "I tend to tiptoe around the edges of any church I happen to see. But I'll oblige y'all with a story, just to show I'm so very thankful for the hospitality and the vittles!"

Cheers and shouts of encouragement followed. Spoon Man cleared his throat and shifted to the edge of his chair. Then he began, his voice low and deep.

"Once, long, long ago, there was a noble eagle who laid three eggs. She carefully set them in her nest atop the tallest mountain. She watched those eggs, and kept them warm, and loved her little nestlings even before they hatched.

"But one day a great storm raged around that mountaintop. The winds blew something fierce, and heavy rains pelted the eagle and her nest. Thunder crashed and lightning crackled! An earthquake rocked the earth. Why, the whole world shook with the power of that storm!"

As he spoke, Spoon Man whistled like the wind and burbled thunder from his lips, flailing his arms to capture the fury of the tempest. Stella scooted closer to her mother, who very quietly slipped the purple bracelet onto Stella's wrist. Her first bracelet! Stella laced her fingers between her mother's.

"The mother eagle did all she could to protect her eggs," Spoon Man continued, "but during the height of the storm, one of those eggs was blown out of the nest, and it rolled swiftly down that mountain. The mother eagle squawked and cried out, but there was nothing she could do except try to protect the two eggs that remained. The storm ended, the rains stopped, the sun came out, but the egg was gone and the mother eagle was heartbroken.

"Now that egg that fell didn't break. No, M'am and no, sir! It came to rest in the garden of a farm at the base of the mountain.

"The next morning the farmer noticed the unusual egg. He picked it up and placed it in the nest of his favorite chicken—the Rhode Island Red that took such good care of her chicks."

Stella could almost imagine going out to check her chickens for eggs and finding a big old eagle egg sitting there. Yep, that's just what she would do—give it to her best hen.

Spoon Man cleared his throat. Mrs. Hawkins brought him a glass of lemonade. He gulped some down and continued.

"That mother hen, she clucked a little, but she made room for the eagle egg in her nest. A few days later—*scratch, scratch, peep, peep*. Three little chickens poked their way out of their shells, and for the next few days they happily began exploring the farmyard while the mother hen stayed with the last egg, the big one.

"On the fifth day, the strange, large egg began to shudder and crack until a gigantic chick emerged from that shell, wide-eyed, and doin' more squawkin' than peepin'. Gradually it, too, began to explore the farmyard and joined its brother and sisters as they all learned how to be chickens. They learned to drink water from the pan the farmer had set out for them, how to pick up little pieces of grain with their beaks, and how to scratch in the dirt for bugs or grubs. They followed their mother around as she taught them how to survive.

"The three little chicks were a pretty golden-yellow color, but the larger chick was pure white with large, dark curious eyes. His beak was black instead of yellow, and so were his claws. He was a clunky, awkward little fella. But the mama chicken didn't mind at all—she loved him and took care of him no matter what."

Spoon Man took another sip of the lemonade.

"As the chicks got older, the baby eagle grew increasingly discontented. While his sisters grew to be plump yellow chickens, and his brother into a rusty red-rooster, the baby eagle had lost the white feathers and turned into a sleek golden-brown bird—so much taller and stronger than the other chickens.

"His brother and sisters either ignored him or

laughed at him as he scratched for food. The mama tried to intervene when she could, but she knew that children had to find their own way.

"Finally, one bright clear day, the young eagle looked up and saw something soaring high above. It was sleek and black. It glided on the currents of the wind, swooping and turning with the breeze.

"'Oh my,' said the young eagle. 'I wish I could do that.'

"His brother the rooster cackled, 'You can't do that. You're a *chicken*! And everybody knows that chickens don't fly in the sky.'

"The young eagle tucked his head in his wings and scratched in the dirt sorrowfully. The mama chicken walked in that funny chicken strut over to him. 'Son,' she asked, 'do you want to fly?'

"'Oh yes! I wish I could fly like that great bird I saw in the sky. I wish it more than anything.'

"'Then you must fly,' the mother chicken said simply.

"'But I can't! I'm a chicken!'

"'No, son,' she said. 'You have never been a chicken. And you have always been meant to fly. Now get up on that stump!'

"The little eagle leaped for the stump. He fell down in the dirt. He jumped again. And fell once more. Then he did something he'd never tried before. He unfurled his wings and flapped as he jumped. And to his shock and delight, he felt himself lift into the air, higher than he could jump. He landed on the stump with ease and looked back at mama chicken wide-eyed.

"'Good-bye, my child,' the mama chicken said tearily. 'Find your family. Find your destiny. Find your wings!'

"The young eagle flew effortlessly to the top of the fence, then to the roof of the house. He looked at the wide blue sky, took a deep breath, and leaped off. The wind caught him as he spread his wings to their full expanse and soared! He glided and swooped! He did turns and circles and somersaults. He screeched in delight." Spoon Man was now standing—his own arms stretched out, his face turned to the night sky.

Then he dropped his voice to a whisper. "And you know who heard that sound?" He looked at the children. "The mama eagle. Mothers always know the voice of their children."

Every mother in the circle gave a little hug to her closest child.

Spoon Man settled back down in his chair. "The mother eagle flew out to meet him with great joy and brought him back to the top of the mountain, where he belonged.

"'I'm an eagle,' the young bird said triumphantly. 'And I was born to fly!'"

At that moment, Stella almost felt like she could fly herself.

⋆15⋆
The Unseen River

It took hours for Stella's family to fall asleep that night. Stella had helped her mother clean up after all the guests had left. Then she helped her father set up a pallet in the barn for Spoon Man. And although Stella thought Jojo would have been exhausted from all the excitement, he tossed and turned until late in the night. Stella had to fight to stay awake.

Finally she slipped on her father's jacket and snuck outside. The fire pit still held the glow of the fading logs, but it offered very little heat.

She wasn't gonna be able to do this much longer—it was cold! Sneaking out here to write didn't seem to be helping her writing in school anyway, she thought glumly, tucking her toes under the hem of her nightgown. In addition to the cold, her deep sense of unease was back, without the laughter and stories from earlier to chase it away.

She thought about Spoon Man's tale of the eagle, and his advice about writing away the worries, but mostly she just gazed at the stars and brooded about flight and birds and airplanes, which she'd seen exactly only four times in her entire life as they zoomed across the sky.

So she nearly jumped out of her skin when the door opened. It was just her mother. She plopped down beside Stella and wrapped the blanket from Stella's bed around them both.

"You know I see you every time you sneak out at night," her mother said, pulling her close.

"You do?"

"There's not much around here that a mama misses."

"I guess not," Stella said, thinking back to what Mama had said about her grandmother not sleeping for twenty years. "It's just that . . . well, I like the night. And it's a good place to hide."

"Hide? From what?"

Stella inched away, making a face. "I come out here to practice, Mama. I've got stuff in my head, but I don't know how to get it out. I try to write it down sometimes, but I'm not very good at it. It's like my brains are dumplings in somebody else's soup." She looked up toward the stars, but even the sky had turned murky.

Her mother hugged her closer. "I've talked to Gertrude Grayson a time or two," she said gently.

Stella stiffened. *Betrayed!*

"She says you are the best thinker in the school."

"Really? I guess she also told you how I been messin' up."

Mama stroked Stella's hair. "You remember when I planted those strawberries a few years back? You must been about Jojo's age."

"Yeah."

"The first year they came up sour and pink."

"I remember. I tasted a couple, and I couldn't spit them out fast enough—so sour my tongue wanted to shrivel up and leave!"

Mama nodded. "The next season I had enough ripe red ones to fill a pail and make a pie—long as I added sugar!" She paused. "But this past season—I know you remember, 'cause I couldn't keep you away from them—they were so sweet and thick they made ordinary sugar be 'shamed."

"Yes, but—"

"Your time to blossom sweet is comin', Stella. But I don't want you outside at night anymore, you hear? It's just not safe."

"Yes'm." After a bit, Stella said, "Tonight was fun. It was kinda nice having the whole neighborhood around. And nobody seemed too scared."

"You know, back in slavery times, our people told stories and sang songs to pass on information when it was dangerous to say things out loud."

Stella considered that—she'd been told that before, but she'd actually never *really* thought about it. "Kinda like Papa's newspapers, huh?"

"A little. There's an unseen river of communication that forever flows—dark and powerful. Tonight was about food and laughter, yes. But it was also about navigatin' that river."

A dog barked in the distance. Stella listened close, but all else was quiet, so she said, "You know what I've been thinkin' about, Mama?"

"What's that?"

"I really liked Spoon Man's story, but I kept thinking about stuff like why chickens can't fly or why eagles live on mountaintops. I'd love to go the library in Spindale and read a book about how *anything* flies— that would be incredible."

"I'm sure books like that exist . . . ," her mother said carefully.

"But I'm not allowed to use the library." Stella's eyes flashed as she finished her mother's sentence. "I know. And it's just not fair!"

Her mother brushed her lips against Stella's ear. "Perhaps one day things will change."

"Not if the Klan has anything to do with it," Stella replied, twirling the new bracelet on her wrist. "I really like the bracelet, Mama. I know you could have used that money for something more important."

"Every girl needs something pretty in her life, something special to make her smile," her mother said. "But far more important than a glass trinket, Stella, is the joy you already got in you."

"I got something else special, Mama. . . ." Her mother waited, and Stella reached down and pulled out the cigar box full of clippings. "Did you know about this, too?" she asked, opening it up.

Sounding amused, her mother told her, "I've wrapped quite a bit of garbage recently in newspapers with holes cut out of them. But I know the value of a secret."

Stella gave Mama her school notebook, the one that held the paper marked with a F, the incomplete assignments that sat there like half-plowed furrows, the jumble of scribbles and thoughts.

Mama flipped through it all, squinting as the clouds continued to obscure the stars.

Stella held her breath.

"Gertrude is right," Mama said finally.

"I'm a dunce?" Stella said, fear clutching her chest.

"Quite the opposite. You are an amazing thinker—a gemstone hiding inside a rock."

"So how come all I can feel is the rock?"

"What I'm reading here is thoughtful and beautiful, just like you are."

"More like thick and tangled, like my hair," Stella mumbled. She did, however, take the notebook into the house with her. "Would it be all right if I try to write a little something before I go to sleep?" she asked. "Maybe I can scribble some ideas while my brain is not feeling so fried."

Mama touched Stella's cheek. "Sure, baby. But not for long. We got church in the mornin'."

Stella plopped down by the embers of the fire. She smiled. Because words were starting to make sense. Bright, perfectly formed ideas smoldered in her mind. She opened her notebook.

★ 16 ★
Up in the Air

UP IN THE AIR

I don't know how airplanes stay up in the air and fly. It must really be something to sit inside an airplane, then look out the window (I guess they have windows!) and see clouds underneath you instead of above like they are ~~suppozd~~ supposed to be.

I don't know how birds fly either. How can a clump of feathers with legs and wings take off and just float on a breeze? Their brains are much smaller than mine, but they know how to fly, and I don't. ~~I guess birds know more than I do about what clouds look like up close.~~

Spoon Man talked about eagles and what their wings look like when they fly. Sometimes they are brown with white tips on the end. The pastor wears wing-tipped shoes every Sunday. That's the first time I understood why folks call them that!

★ 17 ★
I Am a Man. Amen.

Mama was already stoking the fire, sweeping the floor, and warming up a few leftovers from the potluck meal when Stella woke up. She reached under her pillow and touched the notebook she'd tucked there before she fell asleep. She got up and dressed quickly, hurrying to help.

Spoon Man knocked on the door, jarring Jojo awake. "I come to bid you good-bye, Mills family," he said. "Much obliged for your hospitality, your friendship, and your food."

"And thank *you* for the stories, Mr. Oglethorpe. How about a cup of coffee and a biscuit for the road?" Stella's mother asked.

"Why, yes, M'am. That'd be right nice," Spoon

Man replied, easing himself into a chair.

As she poured his coffee, Mama asked, "You're gonna stop by church services before you get on the road, aren't you?"

Stella smirked. Despite the late night, she knew that her mother would be extremely upset if *any* of them even thought about missing church this morning.

"Well, now that you mention it, I suppose I will do exactly that, Miz Mills. Nothin' better than a good sermon to send a man safely on his journey." As her mother went to get the bread, he winked at Stella. "I shoulda left before dawn!" he whispered.

Though the church was almost within walking distance, Papa always hitched Rudie, their mule, to the wagon for the trip to New Hope Church. It had been built some fifty years back, hidden in the woods, right near the river just in case somebody needed baptizing. About three-quarters of the colored families went to New Hope. The rest went to the Galilee Mountain Church, on the other side of town.

Stella's father helped her mother climb onto the seat up front, and Stella smiled. She loved it when her father was gallant like that.

Jojo sat in the back with Stella, busying himself with a bag of marbles, sorting them by color and importance.

"I will not see one single marble during the service, is that clear?" Mama warned without even turning around.

"Yes'm," Jojo said, putting the sack into a pocket.

Stella felt especially dressed up this morning wearing the new glass bracelet. She turned her wrist in the air, the purple jewels glinting in the sunlight.

Even from a distance, Stella thought their church was the prettiest in the county. It had been freshly whitewashed that summer, and flowers circled the wooden cross that stood in the front. The cross was mighty unusual—it was crooked. It had been struck by lightning a few years back, and the pastor had said it was a sign from heaven, like a blessing, and that they ought to leave it just like that. And so they did.

Stella waved as they passed her friends. Most of the families were either walking or riding in wagons. Only one had a car—Mrs. Odom and Claudia. But Mrs. Odom rarely drove it, not even to church. She kept it in her barn, covered with blankets.

The Spencer family were walkers. The line of them stretched down the road for what seemed like a mile as all fifteen ambled toward the church. Mrs. Spencer carried Hetty, the youngest. Hannah, the oldest, who was eighteen, held the hands of the three-year-old twins Horace and Harold. The rest, in stiff-starched dresses and trousers, marched behind. They filled up two entire pews. The Mills family usually sat directly behind the Spencers.

The thing Stella liked best about church was that it was not quite perfect. There was, of course, the cross out front. But also, the piano was always just a little off-key. The ladies in the choir weren't always in tune. The building was too hot in the summer and too cold in the winter. The floorboards sagged, and the wooden pews had been rubbed smooth by all the bodies that had slid across them over the years. The pastor usually preached too long, and the hallelujahs sometimes got too loud. *Well, amen anyhow,* Stella thought.

She spied Spoon Man at the far end of the very back pew and smiled to herself, pretty sure that he would be gone before the first song was over.

After the songs and the prayers, Pastor Patton

finally went to the pulpit to preach. His long white robe swirled around him, and the morning sun shone through the front window, so he almost appeared to glow. Stella giggled and whispered to Jojo, "He looks like he just floated down from heaven or something."

Jojo laughed. "I saw him eat last night. That man can throw down some food—angels don't burp like that!"

Their mother shushed them with a finger to her lips, her eyes never leaving the preacher, who was talking about Moses and the Hebrew slaves. Stella had heard sermons about Moses so many times before that she thought *she* could give a Moses sermon. She slouched down in the pew and fiddled with the beads on her bracelet.

Pastor Patton rattled on. "You know, church, we've been using the story of Moses since before slavery times to talk about freedom for our people. And yes, we are no longer slaves. But are we really free? How many of us still owe money to the owner of the general store? How many of us still sharecroppin'? How many of us are *truly* our own men?"

Stella glanced around. More than a few men were

looking down at the floor, shifting in their seats, her father included.

Pastor Patton continued, "All of us have heard about the recent possible threats from the Klan. Are you afraid?" He waited. Nothing. He raised his voice. "I'm asking again—ARE YOU AFRAID?"

Still, nobody spoke up. Mothers looked away to tend to children, and fathers cleared their throats and picked dirt from their fingernails. The same people who, just a few hours before, had been laughing and joking now looked taut and strained.

The pastor then said, his voice gentle, "If you are afraid, then those who foster hatred will win. Is that what you want?"

Stella could feel the tension in the room.

"People of Bumblebee, we have a presidential election coming up next month. This is the year 1932, children. The modern world is upon us. Telephones! Airplanes! Radios! Who knows what will be invented next? I, for one, am excited to be a part of whatever is comin' around the corner." The preacher narrowed his eyes. "How many of us are registered to vote? How many are brave enough to try?"

Old ladies began to fan themselves as if it were the middle of summer. Feet shuffled in place. Pastor Patton, arms raised so his robe looked like wings, reminded Stella of Spoon Man's eagle—perched and waiting.

"I shall be going into Spindale tomorrow morning," he told them. "And I'm fixin' to register to vote. I will be at the voter registration office at nine a.m. when it opens. Anybody who wants to come with me is welcome. I am a man. Amen. Amen."

With that, he sat down. The entire congregation sat stock-still, stunned. Then Sister Hawkins jumped up, called the choir forward, and led them quickly into the old spiritual, "Go Down, Moses." After a shaky start, the altos started harmonizing mellow and deep.

"Go down, Moses
Way down in Egypt's land
Tell old Pharaoh to
Let my people go!"

After one last short prayer, church was quickly dismissed. Usually there was a lot of handshaking and friendly conversation after service, but today everyone hurried out, grabbing their children and rushing to their own homes.

As her family climbed into the wagon, Stella dared to ask, "What are *you* gonna do, Papa?"

"I'm not sure yet, Stella girl," he replied. "What do you think, Georgia?"

"I think I trust every inch of you, Jonah Mills. So I trust you'll make the right decision." Stella's mother sat up tall on the wagon seat, her gaze focused straight ahead.

"What's the sense of living if you're ashamed of yourself?" Stella's father said almost to himself. Then he gave the mule's reins a slap, and they were off.

⋆18⋆
It's Hard to Be a Tree

Later that afternoon Stella could hear the raw sounds of chopping and hacking, the pounding of ax against wood. She glanced out of the window in time to see her father cleave a log into three separate pieces, which he then heaved onto a growing woodpile.

"What you doin', Papa?" she asked, coming out to the porch.

"What's it look like?" he answered gruffly, never losing his rhythm.

"You angry, Papa?" she asked hesitantly.

"Anger never fixed nothin'," her father replied, picking up another fat log.

Thwop! Crack! Brack! Thunk! He attacked the wood relentlessly. Sweat stained the back of his work shirt.

"Know what I think?" Stella said after a few minutes of watching him hack at the wood.

"What?"

"I think it's really hard to be a tree."

"Huh?" Her father paused to wipe his forehead. "Girl, you always got some strange way of talkin' about stuff. What do you mean?"

"A tree starts out thin and small, sort of like . . ." She thought for a moment, then said triumphantly, "Like Jojo. Then it gets tall and strong and green, like *you*, Papa."

He scratched his head. "And?"

"And then, then it's old and gets chopped up for firewood. That's pretty sad." She picked up a split log and walked it over to the stacked wood.

"Maybe," Papa said, leaning on the ax. "But that woodpile over there is now home to mice and bugs and snakes. And it's just waitin' to keep *us* warm. Everything's got its place and time. You gotta look at the big picture, girl."

Stella felt a little befuddled. "Seems like I can *never* find the big picture, Papa."

"If it makes you feel any better, grown-ups often

ain't got the slightest idea what they're doing either!" her father said, putting his arm around her shoulders. "We just figure it out one day at a time. C'mon, let's get ready for supper."

At dinner her parents were oddly quiet, and Stella could tell that tensions were swelling. As soon as he finished his apple pie, Papa grabbed his newspapers, sat down in his favorite chair, and began reading intently.

Jojo headed out to the front yard with the dog, a couple of horseshoes in hand. The familiar ping of steel against steel soon echoed back to the silent house. A look from her mother let Stella know she needed to disappear for a bit as well, and she was glad to do so.

She made for the back door, but spun around and quickly grabbed the notebook and a pencil from under her pillow, glancing briefly at a faded story about the cotton crop on the wall. She sat on the stoop, listening to the voices of her parents rising and falling like stormy winds. Their disagreements were so rare that the world felt a little tilted. But how to write that down and explain it? She had no clue. How do the people who write the newspaper articles find the right words to print?

Stella opened her notebook reluctantly. She thought

about Papa's tree cutting, and the trees from the forest that had stood there probably for centuries. Her thoughts skittered between eagles that learned to fly, and men who were scared to jump off that stump, and Moses who said, "Let my people go." She leaned over and wrote just one word. *Trees.*

She wrote a few sentences. Scribbled them out. Wrote one more. Bit her pencil. Wrote three more—scratched out two. *Dust becomes words.* Hey, that was not so bad. Scrawled out a whole paragraph. Erased half of the next one. What was left was not so bad at all, she decided.

The sun grew golden, then rusty as it slipped slowly toward the horizon. Then, out of the blue, a gaggle of silvery geese erupted from the reeds at the pond's edge, honking and swirling in circular disorder. Stella went instantly alert. What had them all riled up? A fox? It wasn't more of those men, was it? Then she heard a crackling of underbrush—or was it just the random movement of the fallen leaves? There was no way to be sure, but Stella decided not to take any chances. She hurried back into her house, pulled the back door shut, and locked it.

⋆19⋆
Trees

TREES

At the lumber mill they chop up trees
that end up getting turned into furniture
and houses.

Pine trees.

Walnut trees.

Oak and hickory.

Willow is my favorite.

There must be dozens of different kinds
of trees in the woods in the back of our
house. Each kind is different—some with
fat leaves, some with leaves that bloom,
some with spikes or needles.

I wonder what kind of tree I would need

if I wanted to build a boat. Or what tree
would be best for a bow and an arrow. And
how do you figure that out?

How do you know which trees have fruit
that is good for you and which fruit will
~~pioson~~ poison you? I would hate to be the
first person to try.

At the mill, Papa says they take the sawdust
and turn that into paper. Those big old trees
become books and notebooks and newspapers.

Dust becomes words. I like that.

★ 20 ★
The Cow with No Head

Two nights later Stella woke up in the middle of the night to the sound of Jojo screaming. "Not again!" she cried, scrambling out of bed.

"Help!" Jojo shouted, flinging the back door open, racing into the house. "Help!"

Mama, her hair wrapped in paper-bag curlers, and Papa, grabbing his shotgun from above the mantel, reached Jojo just as Stella did.

Jojo clutched the doorknob, breathing hard. He looked terrified.

"What is it, boy?" his father asked. "Did you see the Klan again?"

"No. Worse," Jojo answered breathlessly.

"Worse? What could be—?" Stella started to ask.

"Is somebody hurt?" Mama interrupted, dropping to her knees in front of him.

"No, Mama. It's nothing like that."

"So why in heaven's name are you screaming in the middle of the night, waking everybody up?" Papa asked, his voice a blend of fury and fear.

Jojo looked at them, his face serious. "I got up to tee-tee again—"

"You're gonna have to stop going to the outhouse at night! Use the chamber pot!" Stella exclaimed, cutting him off.

"Stella, let the boy talk," her father admonished.

". . . and I saw a cow with no head!" Jojo buried his head into his mother's flannel nightgown.

"What are you talking about?" his father asked. "There's no such thing!"

"It's in the back, mooing like a cow, even wearin' a bell like a cow, but it ain't got no head! You gotta believe me!"

"Jojo, I think you're dreaming—how can a cow moo without a head?" Stella asked.

"I am *not* making this up," Jojo insisted.

Mr. Mills brushed the boy out of the way and headed outside.

"See?" Jojo said, pointing.

Cloud cover made the night moonless, and the dark felt thick. "Mwooo," a cow bellowed. Stella could hear the clanking of its bell and the sound of it bumping into things. It seemed confused.

"You see?" Jojo insisted, standing tucked behind Stella.

Stella peered into the darkness, and yes, she could clearly see the shape of a cow, and yes, it seemed to have no head!

Their father, though, solved the whole mystery in a second. He approached the frightened animal. "Sh-sh-sh, now. It's gonna be all right," he murmured. He grabbed the rope around the cow's neck and led it closer to the house. "It's the Winstons' cow," he explained to Jojo, sounding half-exasperated, half-amused.

Stella laughed out loud. "It's not headless—it's a white cow with a black head, you little featherbrain!"

"You've seen this cow next door a million times, Jojo," Mama said, starting to laugh herself.

"But it *did* look like it had no head," Jojo insisted.

"In the darkness, I suppose it did," his mother

agreed, small bursts of laughter escaping from her lips.

"I'm sorry I woke everybody up again," Jojo said, now sounding miserable. "But I was really scared."

"With Klan folks burning crosses in the middle of the night, we don't need frights over cows, Jojo, you hear?" Papa scolded. "You holler when there's *real* danger. Otherwise, keep your mouth shut!" Although his voice was stern, Stella could see that even he was trying to keep his face from breaking into a smile.

As Jojo shifted from one foot to the other, Papa told him, "You'll be taking this cow back to its own barn before daylight. They will be missing her, and she'll be needin' a milkin'."

"Yes, sir," Jojo said.

"Can't get a lick of sleep around here," their father groused as they all trooped back into the house. But he put his arm around his wife, and Stella could hear them murmuring with amusement as they climbed back to the loft.

Stella motioned for Jojo to come sit beside her at the table. "Chin up, Jojo. We needed something to make us laugh around here."

"I feel kinda stupid," Jojo admitted. "But I was *soo* scared!"

"Don't feel bad. Lotsa stuff scares me, too."

"Like what? You never act like you're afraid of nothin'."

"Snakes. Bears. Worms in apples. Toenail clippings. Floods. I could tell you dozens of things."

"Really?"

"Trust me. The older you get, the scarier the world gets to be."

"That's s'posed to make me feel better?"

"No, that's s'posed to make you understand the real deal." She gave him a big hug. "And *that*," she said, "is to let you know I will be there for you. No matter what."

"You scared of getting beat at checkers?" he asked slyly.

"Not a chance, youngun! Even though it's the middle of the night, I'll still roast you. Get ready to suffer!"

So instead of going back to bed, Jojo ran to get the checkerboard.

⋆ 21 ⋆
Papa's Standing Stone

The next morning, as Stella was washing up out at the pump, her father joined her, a strange look on his face.

"What's wrong, Papa?" she asked warily.

"Nothing. Just—you're not going to school today."

Stella froze, water dripping from her face. "Why not?"

"I'm fixin' to register to vote, and I want you to be there," her father said gruffly.

"Me?"

"You're my oldest child, you got smarts enough to be somethin' special like a teacher or a doctor one day." Her father paused and cleared his throat. "I need you to be my standing stone, to be my strength this day."

Papa's standing stone! Stella felt mighty nervous, but excited at the same time. And missing a day of school? Who wouldn't jump at the chance? She dressed quickly, then brushed and braided her hair extra tight.

Her mother gave her a piece of warm biscuit and a hug before they left. "Stones don't cry, child. Remember that," was all she said.

Stella rarely had the chance to go anywhere alone with her father, and now she was on her way to Spindale—just the two of them. It would probably be a forty-minute ride on the wagon. If they had a horse, it would be quicker—the mule was slow. But as Papa always said, riding with old Rudie was better than walking!

Her father was quiet for the first few miles, and Stella did not disturb his pensive mood. Finally he said, "You know, Stella, when I was eleven, I had to quit school. Grandaddy needed me to work in the fields."

"I think about that, Papa, and it makes me feel"— she paused, glancing up at him—"kinda sad. You know, school is sometimes, well, not so easy for me, but I'd hate to be told I couldn't go."

Her father shook the reins to hurry Rudie along. "I understand, Stella girl."

"How'd you get so smart if you didn't go to school?" Stella asked.

"Well," Papa said, "not goin' didn't stop me from learnin'. The teacher brought books by my house every week, and I read every last one of them when we quit workin' for the day. I read by firelight. I used to study by starlight, too, just like you do."

"And I thought it was my big secret!" Stella said, covering her head with her arms and laughing.

"You think I ain't aware of every creak and squeak in that house? That I don't know every single second what every member of my family is doing?" He fixed her with a look. "I didn't just fall off the turnip truck, girl! But here's the thing, Stella," her father continued, "I don't want you out there at night anymore. Too dangerous."

"Yes, Papa. Mama already told me."

He gave one of her stubby pigtails a pull. "Sometimes even children can be targeted. I pray that times get better for your young ones. And for theirs."

At this, Stella couldn't suppress a snicker.

"I don't see nothin' funny about what I just said!"

"I was just thinking about me having children. Or being a grandma!" She giggled. "Think I'll be fat and have gray hair?"

"I sure hope so," her father said, laughing himself. After a few miles he asked Stella, "So, what do you have to write about so badly that you be sneakin' around my house at all hours of the night?"

"I go out there to practice, Papa."

"Practice? For what?"

Stella looked away from him and stared at the thick forest of pines that framed the road like whispering dark-green walls.

"I don't write so good," she admitted. "I can never get the words to sound like I want them to. So I come outside when I can be all alone, and I write stuff that nobody sees."

Her father picked an apple out of the lunch pail Mama had fixed for them. He took a big bite and chewed it before answering. The only sounds were the clomp of the mule's feet and the angry fussing of a pair of squirrels high in a limb above them.

Finally he said, "Bad writers don't practice, Stella. It's the good ones who care enough to try, who worry about getting the words just right. You are probably better than you think."

Stella shook her head, doubtful.

"You know how Tony Hawkins sneaks out every chance he gets to run on the track over at the white school?" Papa said.

Stella looked up, surprised. "You know about that, too?"

"The whole neighborhood does," Papa replied, looking right at her. "We keep an eye out for our own. Young Anthony practices because running is in his heart. He runs at night to get better, to improve, to feel the wind on his face."

Stella had never thought about it quite like that. She frowned and tried to find the right words. "But, Papa, you said it yourself, it's in his heart. I'm just trying not be the worst kid at writing in Mrs. Grayson's class."

"Don't be so hard on yourself, child," her father said gently.

She turned her head to find the woodpecker that was making that determined *rat-a-tat*. "You read newspapers all the time, Papa."

"Yeah. So do you."

"Well, somebody had to write all those articles. That's the kind of writing that maybe I might not be so bad at. Stories about people in Bumblebee. Things I find interesting, like birds or snow. Events like Spoon Man coming. Sometimes just what I think about stuff," Stella told him. "Things that are *real*."

"Like on Mama's newpaper walls," her father said, "That's important."

Stella thrilled at his words. He understood!

Again the silence rode with them for a spell.

"I used to like to write," her father admitted after a bit.

"Really?" Stella asked, genuinely surprised. "Can you show me some of it?"

"It's gone. My father thought boys writing was a waste of time, especially what he called girly stuff like poetry, so he tossed it all in the fireplace one day. I saved a couple of pieces in my head, is all."

"Oh." Stella wasn't sure what else to say, but thinking about her father's words being burned, destroyed, made her stomach queasy. "So you remember *some* of it?" she asked hesitantly.

"Maybe." But then he said nothing more.

"Please?" Stella whispered at last. She waited. The sun warmed her shoulders. Her father shifted in his seat and gave Rudie's rein a gentle slap to move him along, then finally said, "My grandmama Maudie died sudden-like. I was twelve. She had six children and five grandchildren, but I was the only one who called her Granny. Everyone else called her Big Ma. I wrote this the day after we buried her." He cleared his throat. "Lord, I ain't said this out loud in many a year.

"I remember my granny's home cookin',
She'd hum, and she'd mix, and she'd stir.
She could make buttered bones taste delicious,
If that's all the fixin's there were.

I remember my granny's lap-naptimes,
Where memories wrapped in her arms.
She would sing of old pain and lost glory,
Of the long-ago days on the farms.

I remember my granny's old washtub;
It was battered and made out of tin.

Hot suds and toy boats into battle,
Then nighttime and dreams could begin.

I remember my granny's soft blankets,
On a large, squeaky, four-poster bed.
The faint smell of mothballs and cedar,
And her warm breathing close to my head."

Then he called out to Rudie to get along now, and Stella kept her eyes on the trees standing sentinel as they passed. She was wise enough to say nothing.

★22★
Their Declaration of Independence

As they got closer to town, the trees became more spread out, the birdsong stopped, and the road got busier with wagons and even a couple of automobiles.

Stella broke the pleasant silence between them. "So, Papa, *why* are you going to register today? The pastor talked about being scared. Aren't you?"

Her father looked up at the sky—clouds were rolling in from the west. "Of course I'm a little scared. But I'm doing this for my family, for you and your brother. I gotta show that I am somebody—no one else is gonna do that for me."

Stella reached over and placed her small hand on top of Papa's gnarled fingers. She'd never felt so proud.

He nodded his head slightly, then clicked at the mule to move along.

It was startling to Stella how busy a small city could be—the cars, the buildings, the people acting like they had important things to do. She wondered what it would be like to live in such a bustling place.

They pulled up in front of a building with a large window in front. BOARD OF ELECTIONS was neatly painted on the glass in white lettering. Under that Stella read, REGISTER TO VOTE HERE.

Pastor Patton and Mr. Spencer were already there, wagons cleaned, waiting. Mr. Spencer wore a pair of stiffly starched and ironed overalls—probably pretty uncomfortable. The preacher was dressed in a fresh white dress shirt and Sunday slacks. He even wore a tie. "I don't know that anyone else from the congregation is going to join us, men," the pastor said in a low voice. He looked at Mr. Spencer. "Are your children taken care of, Hobart?"

"Yes, sir. My wife is what the Cherokee call Earth Mother. The children are fine. We sent all but the little ones to school today."

"And you, Jonah? Is your family behind you on this?"

Stella's father hesitated. "Georgia supports me, but she was a mite trembly this morning. I brought Stella, though." He squeezed her shoulders affectionately. "I don't want to just tell her about bravery—I want to show her what it looks like."

"Then let us pray," Pastor Patton said firmly. Stella noticed a few townspeople slowing down as they passed by; none of the faces looked pleasant. She closed her eyes. "Dear Lord," said the pastor, "we bow down before you as we stand up for dignity. Be with us and protect us both morning, noon, and night. Amen."

Papa tucked in his shirt and brushed a speck off his shoes. Stella was all the more aware of her bare feet, but she walked in with as much dignity as she could when the pastor opened the door to that office.

"What y'all boys want?" a burly, bearded man asked as they approached his desk. The man's shirt was wrinkled and stained with sweat under the arms, and Stella could see bits of the egg he must have had for breakfast in his beard. A metal name plate sat on his desk in front of a large pile of papers, both typed and handwritten—AMHERST PINEVILLE, REGISTRAR.

Stella's father stiffened at the word "boys," his face

going hard, but Pastor Patton told the man calmly, "We have come to register to vote in the presidential election to be held on November eighth."

"Too late," Mr. Pineville said with a shrug. "Registration done closed a month ago."

Pointing to a sign above the man's head, the pastor said patiently, "That there poster says today is the last day of registration, and we are here to register."

Mr. Pineville sighed. "Do *all* of y'all know how to read?"

"Yes, sir. We read that poster, didn't we?" Mr. Spencer replied, his voice tinged with anger.

"Watch it, boy," Mr. Pineville warned. "Does Sheriff Sizemore know y'all are here in town causin' trouble?"

"We are not causing trouble, and I'm sure the sheriff has more important things to do than worry about where we are spending our day," Stella's father replied.

Another sigh. "Can y'all write?"

"Yes, sir—all of us," Pastor Patton said evenly.

"You gotta pay a fee," the registrar warned.

"We are prepared to pay." Papa's reply was as even as the pastor's.

"And you gotta pass a test—about the Constitution of the United States."

"We teach our children about the Constitution and the Declaration of Independence in our schools," Stella's father said. "That's how we know about our rights."

Mr. Pineville tapped his pencil against his desk, his eyes narrowing. "Y'all ain't deservin' of no rights."

"This is my eleven-year-old daughter, Stella," her father said, placing his hand on her shoulder. "Stella, can you recite for Mr. Pineville here what you learned in school last week?"

"You mean that section of the Declaration of Independence that Mrs. Grayson had us memorize?"

"Yes, child. Show the man."

Recitation was a huge part of the lessons at her school. Even the little ones could rattle off long passages from the Bible, the Declaration, and the Constitution. Stella took a deep breath and spoke without hesitation.

"'We hold these truths to be self-evident, that all men are created equal, that they are endowed by their creator with certain unalienable rights, that among these are life, liberty, and the pursuit of happiness. That to secure these rights, governments are instituted among men, deriving their just powers from the consent of the governed. That whenever any form of government becomes destructive of these ends, it is the right of the people to alter or to abolish it, and to institute new government, laying its foundation on such principles and organizing its powers in such form, as to them shall seem most likely to effect their safety and happiness.'"

Her father beamed. Stella tried not to show how satisfied she felt.

"So what?" Mr. Pineville smirked, seemingly unimpressed. "I've seen a trained monkey that can count to three!"

"My daughter is not an animal, sir," her father said sharply.

"You watch your tone, boy, or I'll throw all of y'all out of here," Mr. Pineville warned. He pulled three sheets of paper from the pile in front of him. "Answer these questions. You got fifteen minutes. And don't be gettin' any answers from your pet monkey!" He leaned back and laughed.

Stella swallowed hard. She'd never been called an animal before. She certainly wasn't going to let that man make her cry, however, so she focused on her father's bushy eyebrows, so like her own. She bit her lip and stared at those eyebrows, and those brown eyes beneath them that looked at her with such love and assurance. *I am a stone. I am a stone,* she thought fiercely.

The heat had risen on her father's face as well, but Pastor Patton firmly guided him to a counter on the far wall before he could respond. There was nothing to write with at the counter.

Mr. Spencer dug into his pants pocket and pulled out three pencils. "I come prepared," he said with a shrug.

Stella leaned over and read some of the questions as her father went through the test.

1. Name the attorney general of the United States.

2. What is a tribunal?

3. What is a treaty?

4. What officer is designated by the Constitution to be president of the Senate of the United States?

5. Write the preamble of the Constitution of the United States.

While the three men wrote their answers, two others, white men, sauntered into the office. "Hey,

Amherst," the tall, skinny one said. Stella recognized him. He was one of those fellows who was always sitting on the benches outside the general store in Bumblebee, playing checkers or sleeping. He liked to yell at her and her classmates as they left the candy store, sometimes calling them names.

"Well, if it ain't Johnny Ray Johnson! What y'all up to?"

"Me and Maxwell Smitherman here come to sign up to vote."

Stella tried not to stare. Mr. Smitherman! He was a foreman at the mill. She took in his patent-leather shoes and his gold pinkie ring. So this was the man her father's friends complained about—his unfairness and downright meanness. Why, he was the one who made Mr. Winston, who had showed up one minute late to work one day, take a load of logs out of a wagon and carry them on his back instead. It had taken him long past midnight to finish. None of the other men had been allowed to help.

"That's my job," Mr. Pineville was saying amiably. "Just sign your name on this here form, and you're all set!"

"That's it?" asked the man called Maxwell.

"That's it. Just sign on this here line, and I'll see you on Election Day."

Stella's father instantly shot an angry look in Mr. Pineville's direction. The pastor frowned at him, and he returned to the test reluctantly.

But the man named Johnny Ray was now staring at *them*. "What you got goin' here this morning—coon school?" he asked.

Mr. Pineville and Mr. Smitherman laughed. "Naw, they think they gonna vote next month. They takin' the test."

"You ever have one of 'em pass it?" Mr. Johnson asked.

Mr. Pineville guffawed. "Most of the time they too stupid to write their names."

Maxwell Smitherman strolled over and poked Mr. Spencer in the side. "Ain't you s'posed to be over at the mill sweepin' up, boy?"

Mr. Spencer raised his chin. "I took the morning without pay, sir," he managed to say. "I aim to work overtime tonight to make up for it."

Smitherman snarled, "Don't plan for any pay for the rest of the week, boy! You don't choose your hours—I do!"

"Yes, sir," Mr. Spencer choked out. Stella could tell

he was about to explode, but Pastor Patton placed a calming hand on his shoulder.

Smitherman must have tired of harassing them, because he abruptly turned and headed for the door. "Keep up the good work, Amherst!" he called out.

But just before he and Johnny Ray left, Stella saw Mr. Johnson lean over Mr. Pineville's desk, glance back at the small group at the counter, and say just loud enough for Stella to hear, "See you at the triple K meetin' tonight." Then they went out the door, talking loudly about a planned fishing trip.

Sudden goose bumps covered Stella's arms. She glanced at her father. She knew they all had heard exactly what she had. But they continued to concentrate on the test, the scratching of their pencils failing to drown out the pounding of her heart. *The Ku Klux Klan. The Ku Klux Klan.*

Another minute of scratching, and all three completed the examination. They gave their pencils to Mr. Spencer and handed the papers back to Mr. Pineville, who tossed them carelessly on his desk.

"That'll be two dollars. Each."

Stella gulped. *Two dollars? Each?* Two dollars could

buy enough cornmeal and flour and sugar to keep her family going for a couple of weeks! Then a thought struck her. Those white men! Why, they hadn't been asked to pay a dime!

Mr. Spencer had a house full of children. He'd surely get less this week at his job at the mill, assuming he still *had* a job when Mr. Smitherman returned to work, she thought furiously. And Pastor Patton's salary came from the collection basket, which usually only gathered a few coins each Sunday, supplemented by the goodness of others who occasionally brought him fresh chickens or eggs or bread.

Her father and Pastor Patton gave two wrinkled dollars apiece to Mr. Pineville without blinking.

Mr. Spencer handed the man a two-dollar bill. "I want a receipt for my money," he said quietly.

Mr. Pineville looked surprised. "Why?"

"I got thirteen children to take care of," he told Mr. Pineville. "I aim to show them the power of a two-dollar bill."

"You don't need to be voting! You are wasting your money, boy! Next thing I know you'll be asking for charity to feed those children."

"I am not a boy. I am a man. And I want a receipt," Mr. Spencer stated firmly.

Stella held her breath.

Mr. Pineville scowled, then busied himself sorting papers, but at last he got out his receipt book and scribbled out what Mr. Spencer had requested.

"Thank you," Mr. Spencer said as he folded the receipt and tucked it into the bib of his overalls.

"When do we find out if we passed the test?" Pastor Patton asked.

"Come back in a week," Mr. Pineville told them.

"I'd like to know now, sir," Stella's father said.

"I told you—come back in a week," Mr. Pineville insisted.

"Those other two men didn't have to take a test to register to vote." Stella was impressed at her father's nerve.

Mr. Pineville shrugged. "Them's *white* rules."

Mr. Spencer cocked his head. "Do you even know the answers to the test?"

"Well . . . well . . . of course I know the answers!" Mr. Pineville sputtered.

"So grade them. Now." Mr. Spencer sat down on

the floor. After a moment, Stella's father and Pastor Patton joined him.

Mr. Pineville dropped his pencil. "What you doin' on the floor?"

"Waiting for you to grade the test," Mr. Spencer replied.

"I'll call the sheriff if you don't get out of here," the registrar warned, standing up.

"No need to involve the law. We just want the tests graded. Now. Please," Pastor Patton added.

Stella sank to the dusty floor beside them, sliding close to her father.

Mr. Pineville was clearly perplexed. "I'm extremely busy today," he said.

"We understand. We'll wait," Mr. Spencer said. "Don't mind us."

"You're gonna be *real* sorry you did this," Mr. Pineville warned.

"Sorrow is part of life," Pastor Patton replied. Then he started to sing, ever so softly.

"Nobody knows the trouble I've seen
Nobody knows my sorrow

Nobody knows the trouble I've seen
Glory hallelujah!"

Her father and Mr. Spencer soon joined in—low, quiet, respectful. Gradually Stella added her own voice—higher, sweeter.

"Sometimes I'm up, sometimes I'm down
Oh, yes, Lord
Sometimes I'm almost to the ground
Oh, yes, Lord

Nobody knows the trouble I've seen
Nobody knows my sorrow
Nobody knows the trouble I've seen
Glory hallelujah!"

When the song ended, they hummed the tune quietly, over and over and over.

Finally Mr. Pineville threw up his arms. "All right! I'll grade 'em. Just quit that awful singing!"

As they fell silent, Stella heard rain plinking steadily on the tin roof of the building.

She also observed that it seemed to take Mr. Pineville a long, long time to read each question and response. He squinted, put on a pair of glasses, then took them off again. He looked at each test paper over and over, moving his lips as he read. And it dawned on Stella that he couldn't read very well!

She took turns watching the clock and watching Mr. Pineville. Forty-seven minutes passed—thirty-five more than it had taken to take the test!

He finally looked up. "Y'all passed. All of you. Now get out of here!"

Stella helped her father up from the floor. The three men exchanged glances—the looks were brief, but loaded. "Thank you, sir," Pastor Patton said.

As they reached the door, Mr. Pineville called out, his voice low and ominous, "You know that song you was singin' about trouble? Be on the lookout for it, 'cause it's comin'."

⋆23⋆
A True Story

Scattered rain followed them all the way home, but even though she was damp and her backside was a little sore from sitting on the wagon seat, Stella was in a good mood. At supper she chattered on to Jojo and Mama all about the trip. Papa remained quiet and thoughtful.

After helping her mother clear the kitchen, Stella hurried to find her notebook. For the very first time, she wanted to write something, and it wasn't an assignment. It wasn't required. She just wanted to remember what Papa had told her.

THE MAN WHO WANTED TO BE A SOLDIER

A TRUE STORY

Today I rode into town with Papa, and he told me a story I never heard before. When Papa got old enough, he ~~wanted to~~ decided to join the army. It was 1914. There was a war. Young Jonah wanted to serve his country and go fight the ~~enemy~~ enemy, whoever that was.

The local folks made a big deal about wanting boys from around here to sign up. Somebody said newspaper reporters with cameras would be at the ~~sign-up~~ recruiting office to snap a picture of the first ~~boy~~ young man from our area to ~~sign up to be a soldier~~ enlist.

So my daddy, who had just turned ~~18~~ ~~eighteen~~ eighteen years old, got up ~~early~~ before daylight and walked ~~all the way to Spindale~~ to town. He was the very first in line. ~~Lots of~~ Twenty-two young men showed up that day, but Papa got there first.

When the reporters saw that a colored boy stood first in line, they pushed him out

148

of the way and said he was in the wrong line. ~~and told him to go home.~~

The newspaper people snapped their bright camera bulbs and took ~~lots of~~ dozens of pictures of Jimmy Winkleman, a white boy, instead. He had stood second in line behind Papa.

They ~~wood~~ would not let Papa be in the army. So he walked back home, so very sad. It's strange to ~~imagen~~ imagine my father being so young, and hard to think about him being so sad.

Jimmy Winkleman, Papa told me, died in the war.

⋆24⋆
Empty, Blue-Lined Paper

Stella had stayed up far too late writing. It had taken her a couple of hours, and it still wasn't right. Plus, she kinda missed the thrill of sneaking out to her porch step. At least she got the story down.

So the next morning she trudged down the road yawning, but forgot her fatigue when she reached her friends, telling them about the trip to Spindale, the test the adults had to take, and how they'd all been treated.

"It made me feel good to see somebody finally stand up against a man like that," she finished up. "Well, actually, we sat down, but it worked!"

At school, once attendance had been taken, Mrs. Grayson began the usual morning routine. "Please rise," she commanded. "Hands on hearts. Face the flag, children."

Stella, with the rest of her class, chanted loudly and clearly, "I pledge allegiance to the flag of the United States of America and to the republic for which it stands, one nation, indivisible, with liberty and justice for all."

She always liked the rhythm of the words of the pledge—it made her feel like she belonged to something important.

After the morning prayer, Mrs. Grayson told them to be seated, as she had an announcement. She held up the front page of the *Carolina Times*. "I found something in here yesterday that I think will be both useful and enjoyable. I'm especially pleased to say this opportunity comes from the newspaper that represents Negro people all over the state." Her voice was edged with excitement. "They are offering a contest for all ages—including schoolchildren."

"What kind of contest?" Tony asked. "Sports?"

"Not this time, Anthony," Mrs. Grayson replied. "The planners of the competition are looking for art and poetry and writing."

Tony thunked his head down on his desk. Stella groaned. *More* writing?

"I do believe, however, that the newspaper sponsors an athletic contest in the spring, Anthony. We'll be sure to participate in that one as well," Mrs. Grayson promised. "Now sit up straight!"

Helen Spencer raised her hand. When Mrs. Grayson acknowledged her, she asked, "If we do the writing one, how long does it have to be?"

Looking down at the information in front of her, Mrs. Grayson replied, "The entries may be drawings or stories or essays, no longer than three handwritten pages. And the best pieces will be published in the paper!"

"Do we *have* to enter the contest?" Randy asked. "I like bugs and science better."

"Scientists must be good writers as well," Mrs. Grayson informed him.

"I knew she'd say that!" Carolyn whispered to Stella.

The teacher went on, "Each of you will prepare a piece of writing or art for the contest. I will choose the best from each of the age categories and submit those three to represent Riverside School."

"What will they be judged on?" Carolyn asked.

"Creativity. Clarity. Cleverness. And penmanship! Poor handwriting can destroy your chances to win," Mrs. Grayson replied, looking stern.

"Since I can't *do* a sport in the competition, do you think it's all right if I *write* about sports?" Tony asked.

"I'm sure that will be acceptable," Mrs. Grayson told him. "So let's get busy, children. I expect our Riverside School to be wonderfully represented in this contest! We will spend from now until lunch working on ideas and rough drafts. Little ones—grades one, two, three—I will work with you first. Get your pencils out and ready to draw your very best pictures. Older students—I want you to organize your thoughts, take notes, and decide what you will write."

The room buzzed with activity for the next hour or so. Stella, however, sat slumped in her seat. Everybody else was scribbling away on their papers. Stella stared at her empty, blue-lined sheet, disheartened. She couldn't think of a thing to write about, or anything that anybody else would even want to read. *All that practicing in the middle of the night didn't do me a lick of good!*

Hazel leaned over into the aisle and called out, "Stella? How do you draw a picture of a hole?"

Stella was happy for an excuse to close her notebook. "A hole?"

"Yeah. You know. Like a hidey-place hole. With snakes."

"Snakes?"

"Yep."

"I'm not sure," Stella told her, thinking what a strange thing that was for the first grader to draw for the contest. "I reckon it would be round and dark, right? Why do you want to draw a hole?"

Hazel looked at her as if that was the silliest question in the world. "I've got twelve brothers and sisters," she explained patiently. "When you live in my house, you gotta have a hidey-hole. That's what my story is about. So how do you draw it?"

Stella did the best she could, but she really had no idea how to create the picture that Hazel wanted. When school let out, Hazel thanked Stella and said she'd be able to finish it all by herself the next day.

On the way home, Stella was in no mood to joke or play around with her friends like she usually did.

Most of the boys had stayed late to pitch horseshoes in the school yard, but Tony joined her. Jojo trailed not far behind, picking up rocks and pitching them at tree trunks.

It was a perfect October afternoon, with the sun streaming through what remained of the russet leaves of the maple and beech trees that lined the road. But Stella focused on kicking up clouds from the reddish dirt at her feet instead. She hadn't written a thing for the contest. Not one single word.

"What's got you all cattywampus?" Tony asked her.

"I'm just missin' the summer," Stella replied with a shrug. "Everything gets crunchy and fades away in the fall and winter."

"Me, I like the fall," Tony proclaimed, pretending the tree branch he'd swept up from the side of the road was a sword. "And I like the way you say stuff," he said. "You're not ordinary. And not crunchy," he added.

Stella smiled at him hesitantly. "Thanks, I guess," she said, wondering what being "not crunchy" meant. "I was just thinking about the writing contest and what I can enter." She hoped she didn't sound stupid.

"Words fall out of the sky like leaves, girl. Grab a couple and write 'em down."

"You make it sound so easy," she said, catching an apricot-colored leaf in midair as Tony whacked the mottled white trunk of a birch tree.

"Quit tryin' so hard. Just write what you see, what you think. That's all I do." He scooped up an armful of leaves and showered them over her head.

"Quit it!" she said, brushing dust and specks from her hair, laughing.

"You'll think of something," he said easily, brandishing his stick at an invisible enemy. "But me, I think instead of writing about baseball or football, I'm gonna write about a knight who slays a fire-breathing dragon." He beheaded the dried blooms of a hydrangea bush.

"Sounds like a great idea," Stella told him, steering clear of his pretense at knighthood.

"You could write about dragons too," Tony said, now knighting a small boxwood bush.

"I'm lousy at writing make-believe stories."

Tony tossed the stick aside, wiped his hands on his pants, and faced Stella directly. "So write a true story!" he challenged. "Write about what you saw by the pond!"

"Oh, I couldn't!" Stella declared. "It's too dangerous!"

"Why the heck not? And by the way, did you know the head of the Klan is called a Grand Dragon?"

"He *is*?" Her palms instantly grew sweaty.

"So write your own dragon story. I dare you!" With that, he turned on his heel and ran ahead.

Stella kicked up red dust the whole rest of the way home, wondering if she dared.

⋆25⋆
Dragons

Stella sat on her back steps. Though the sun was going down over the pond, it wasn't dark yet, so no one could scold her.

Should she dare? Should she dare write about the Klan? Sometimes people had to be *ready* for the truth, she decided. She pressed her notebook open flat. Maybe just whispering about the truth at first would be a better idea. She'd be—what did Mrs. Grayson call it? Subtle! She'd be subtle. But she'd do it for the contest.

Three drafts later, most of the scratch-outs and erasures eliminated, she finally put her pencil back in the box.

SLAYING DRAGONS
Dragons are not real. In storybooks, they

are usually blood-red, with shiny scales and sharp teeth. They have long necks and tails that swing hard enough to knock down any soldier. And wings. Dragons in books can fly.

Dragons are always fierce. Brave warriors, dressed in thick armor, go out with shiny swords to slay them. In those stories, dragons are never "killed." They are always "slain" instead—not sure why.

Dragons in fables breathe fire from their mouths. They burn trees and bushes and farmhouses. Castles are harder to burn, I guess, but dragon flames make a really good picture in a storybook.

Knights in armor were real. But dragons—completely made up.

I think the Ku Klux Klan chose the dragon as their symbol because it is scary. The people around here who dress up in bedsheets and call themselves dragons are very real.

But didn't all the dragons from the fairy tales get slain?

⋆26⋆
Chicken Poop and Store-Bought Clothes

Stella *hated* cleaning the chicken coop. Sticky, gooey, stinky poop everywhere. Gummed into the straw, ground into the dirt, stuck in the fencing, flung against the slats of the wall of their enclosure. *How do those dang birds* do *that?* she wondered, scrunching up her nose.

Her mother's boots clomped uncomfortably, even though she had stuffed the toes with old rags. The shovel kept slipping from her hands because Mama's gloves were too big. She *hated* it all. She entered the fenced area and shooed the thankless chickens to one side, blocking them with a large board Papa kept just for cleaning day. They clucked and squawked in protest, but for all Stella cared, they could be made into chicken soup that very minute.

Every other Saturday, this was her chore. She began by shoveling up all the soiled straw and wood shavings and depositing the stinky mess into Papa's wooden wheelbarrow. When it was full, she wheeled the load out to the compost pile and added it to the potato peels, onion skins, apple cores, and every other piece of food garbage that was tossed there every night. *Disgusting!* But Papa used the mess to fertilize everything that grew around the place. And because of that, Mama's tomatoes were the biggest in Bumblebee.

It took several barrows full to finish. Then she had to spread fresh wood chips and straw so the chickens could fill it with poop all over again. Ugh. But at least now it smelled fresh, and the chickens clucked with what she hoped was appreciation when she let them back into that side of the yard.

Mama came out of the house, glanced at the clean chicken area, and told Stella she'd done a nice job.

"Thanks. So do I still have to get all the ripe vegetables from the garden?" she moaned, sagging against the shovel. She was in a mood to trounce Jojo in checkers, not work outside all day. Plus it was *cold!*

"You do if you plan to eat tonight," her mother

retorted. "The spinach will grow well into December if we keep it pruned, and that cabbage by the fence is big enough to pick. You might even find a few bush beans. And pull me some of them collard greens—they'll be great with a few potatoes."

"Aw, Mama," Stella began.

"Quit with your bellyaching, child. I've got fish to clean and fry. You want my job?"

Stella hated touching fish guts even more than coop cleaning. "No, M'am." As she trudged toward the garden, she suddenly grinned with relief. Carolyn Malone was half running up the road, clutching a large book to her chest.

"Good afternoon, Mrs. Mills," Carolyn called out. "We got something really exciting in the mail today! My mother said I could bring it here for a bit to show you." She held out the book and looked over at Stella with a grin of her own.

"Stella's got chores, Carolyn," Stella's mother replied. "You done with yours already?"

"Yes, M'am," Carolyn replied. "If I promise to help Stella finish hers, can me and her look at this for a few minutes? Please? I have to return it soon." The two girls looked at Stella's mother with pleading eyes.

Mrs. Mills glanced at the treasure in Carolyn's arms. "Hmm. This year's Sears and Roebuck catalog," she murmured, wiping her hands on her apron. "That *is* truly special. I haven't seen the fall edition. My, my, my. Well, since it's here, let's take a minute to look at it, girls. Or we can clean the windows!" she added, winking. "Stella, go wash your hands first."

"Thanks, Mama!" Stella tossed the boots and gloves into a corner of the porch and rinsed off in a jiffy. Then she and Carolyn raced inside before Mama could change her mind. Stella pushed three chairs close together while Carolyn carefully placed the catalog on the table.

"Oh, golly," Stella breathed, gingerly touching the thick book.

The cover showed a painting of a white boy, maybe around twelve or thirteen years old, sitting at a desk doing homework. A desk lamp, brass probably, an inkwell, and various papers were placed around him. Behind the boy, as if it was on his wall or maybe in his mind, was a tall, majestic image of George Washington, standing in some clouds and looking serious and presidential. Mrs. Grayson would love that picture.

"That's a painting by Mr. Norman Rockwell," Stella's mother told the girls.

"Who's he?" Carolyn asked.

"A famous painter." Peering closer at the picture, Stella's mother said, "It looks like the boy is writing an essay on Washington, who was born in 1732. 1932 is the two hundredth anniversary—I guess the folks at Sears and Roebuck are celebrating that."

"Even fake boys on catalog covers got writing homework," Stella muttered.

"Did you ever turn in your paper for the contest?" Mama asked.

"Yes, Mama. Yesterday," Stella said, "but it doesn't matter, because mine won't get picked. Now, please, can we turn the page? I want to look at the clothes."

Mama narrowed her eyes but let the subject drop. The three of them marveled over ladies who sported hair curled tightly into the latest bobs, high-heeled shoes, and dresses made of cotton and crepe. The hemlines stopped exactly halfway between the knee and the ankle, and most of the dresses were cinched tight at the waist with belts.

In the children's clothing section, the dresses, worn by smiling blond children, had lace collars and patent-leather belts. One dress, in a pale, sea-green color, made Stella trace its outline with longing. "That dress is just plain beautiful," she whispered.

"A dollar ninety-four for a dress!" Mama exclaimed. "I could buy a whole bolt of cloth for that much."

"Yes, but look how pretty these are," Stella said. "They've got rickrack and buttons and bows."

"You think I can't make a dress that pretty?" her mother asked.

"Oh, I know you can, Mama," Stella said quickly. "It's just the ones in this book are *store-bought!*"

Turning more pages, they came to a full-size sewing machine sitting atop a wooden cabinet with six drawers. "Ahh," Mama said. "Now *that's* a beauty!"

"'Eighteen dollars and seventy-five cents,'" Stella read, shaking her head.

They looked at toys for a quarter, shoes for two dollars, rifles for forty-seven dollars, and even plans for a whole house for one thousand, eight hundred and seventy-four dollars.

"I gotta be rich when I grow up," Carolyn said,

folding her arms. "I gotta have money!"

"Don't aim for riches, child," Mrs. Mills said gently. "Aim for happiness."

"If I get rich, I will be happy!" Carolyn declared.

"Maybe. Maybe not." Mama turned another page, saying, "Just a few more minutes now, Stella. We have chores to complete."

"What would you buy right now if you could?" Stella asked her friend.

"Let's see." Carolyn turned a couple of more pages, then flipped back to earlier in the catalog. "First a bicycle, so I wouldn't have to walk to school. That would only cost me twenty dollars."

"Only."

"Oh, and I'd get a lot of fancy clothes—like Paulette Packard has."

At the name, Stella frowned. Paulette probably never had to play the "what would you buy?" game. She just went out and bought it, most likely.

Carolyn nudged Stella. "How about you?"

"Everything you said," Stella replied slowly, "plus a big, fine house for my family to live in. Then I'd choose books to read—books I can keep. Plus one pretty dress to wear to church. The pale-green one." She stopped Carolyn at the page with the dress she'd loved.

"Ooh, I'll take the blue one," Carolyn added, caressing the dress with her finger.

Stella laughed and paged through the clothing section again, her face slowly growing more serious. Finally she said in a low voice, "Did you notice—I didn't see even one single person who looks like us in this big old book."

"Everybody knows colored folks don't have money to buy the stuff in this catalog," Carolyn reasoned. "It's pretty much a book for white people, so that's who's in it."

Stella looked at her friend in frustration. "But colored people need shoes and hammers and nice dresses. They spend their money too."

"That's why I'm gonna be rich," Carolyn asserted. "So it doesn't matter what color I am."

"Why don't you two take your little colored selves outside and get those bush beans and collards in here before it gets dark," Mama said, edging the book out from under their fingers. "Carolyn, I'm sure Stella would be mighty obliged for the help."

The two girls scurried outside. Like Mama had said, that cabbage was ripe and ready, and they picked the beans and greens in record time. As soon as they were done, they washed their hands extra carefully at the pump to make sure not a speck of dirt would smudge the catalog.

"All done, Mama. May I walk Carolyn home?" Stella asked as Carolyn fetched the book.

"That will be fine. I tell you what, Stella," her mother replied, "run this plate of fish down to Mrs. Bates's place while you're at it, while it's still warm. We have more than we can eat, and it won't keep."

"Yes, M'am." Stella took the plate. "Can I visit at Carolyn's house after I take the fish?"

"For a few minutes. But I want you home before dark. Got that?"

"I will," Stella replied, hurrying out the door after Carolyn.

"Oh, it's getting late," Carolyn said, looking at the sky. The sun would soon be sinking into a dusky evening, like it, too, had been working all day. "I gotta go milk the cow."

"Let me get this plate to Mrs. Bates, then I'll meet

you at the barn," Stella said as both girls picked up speed.

"Well, Stella Mills. How you be, sugar?" Mrs. Bates said as she opened the screen door a few minutes later. She was a thin, tired-looking woman, reminding Stella of a squeezed-out dishrag.

"My daddy caught a huge mess of catfish this morning and we can't eat it all, so Mama sent you some." Stella handed her the plate.

"Bless yo' heart, child. That's right kindly of your mama," Mrs. Bates said, her face lighting up. "Tell her I truly appreciate it. So will my boy Randy—can't seem to keep him filled up these days."

"Tell Randy I said hello," Stella said, "and I'll see him at school on Monday."

"I sho nuff will. He's out back in the woods with Tony Hawkins. They told me they'd be lookin' for coons and snakes and other critters. They best be gettin' back up here 'fore dark," she said, scanning the sky, worry crossing her face.

Stella said her good-byes and started strolling back to Carolyn's when she noticed a strange glow about half a mile ahead. She stopped short—it was like the setting sun, but the bright orange image pulsed and undulated like no sun she'd ever seen. A flicker of fear raced through her as she thought back to the night the Klan had burned the cross. This was a fire, and it seemed a whole lot bigger than that cross. She bit her lip, then realized with a gasp . . . the Spencer house! It was the Spencer house! The Spencer house was on fire!

⋆27⋆
Bucket Brigade

Oh my heavens! The Spencer house. It's burning! Stella could smell it now as well. She broke into a run. At the same time, riding toward her, away from the fire, were three figures on horseback. Bearing down swiftly, dust pluming around them, the horses pounded in her direction. Stella stopped in her tracks, mouth agape.

The horses were nearly upon her, but more terrifying were the horsemen. Each wore a white full-length robe. And a pointed white hood. And each carried a flaming torch in his left hand. The Klan.

Stella scrambled to the side of the road just as they reached her. They reined back to an abrupt halt, the horses snorting and whinnying. Stella could smell the sharp sweat of the heaving animals, the acrid kerosene that kept the flames bright. Even the horses were covered with white sheets, from head to rump.

The tallest rider pointed his torch directly at her. "Tell your daddy and the rest of those boys they were told to expect trouble," he spat out. "The Grand Dragon is watching." Then he added ominously, "Everything will burn." Despite her fear, and despite the fact that the man's voice was muffled through the fabric of the hood, Stella was sure she'd heard it before. And that saddle . . . the saddle was shiny and silver-studded, not worn and brown like the other riders'.

Stella scuttled farther away, stones cutting into her palms. But she never took her eyes from the eyeholes in the face cloth that hung from the man's pointed hood. The man who spoke to her had green eyes— emerald like a summer leaf, but cold as a winter snow. Black saddle. Green eyes. *She knew who he was!*

The man signaled to his cohorts, and in unison, all three horses reared. Stella curled into a tight ball, waiting for the hooves to pummel her, wondering if it would hurt very much when she died. But oh, thank the Lord, thank the Lord, she felt their thunder on the earth beside her. She dared not even peek until she was certain they were far down the road.

Stella wanted to run for help, wanted to run to the Spencers', wanted to run home to her mother. But she couldn't get her body to do any of those things. Her arms pressed against her head, she couldn't move a muscle.

"Stella!" a familiar voice cried. "Stella! Are you hurt? I'll go get my father!"

It was Tony Hawkins, running toward her. A moment later he and Randy were standing over her, their faces strained. Stella couldn't hold it back any longer—she burst into tears, not caring a whit who saw her.

"Is anything broken?" Tony asked.

"No. I'm fine. I'm fine," she said, trying to pull herself together. She pressed her hands against her eyes to stop the tears. *Be a stone! Be a stone!*

She checked to ensure that the men were gone. "It was the Klan. They torched the Spencer house!"

"We saw them! They rode lickety-split right past us," Randy exclaimed, helping her up. "They would have mowed us over if we hadn't gotten out of the way!"

"The Spencers!" Stella cried out. "Their house! It's on fire! We gotta help them!"

A few neighbors were already racing out of their homes, grasping buckets and rushing toward the Spencers'.

"Randy, go to Mrs. Malone's and tell her to use that telephone of hers to call the fire brigade! Hurry!" Tony said. "I'll go get the rest of the families in town to come help."

"You say you could run like the wind, Tony," Stella reminded him. "So run!"

The two boys dashed off away from the fire, and Stella turned on her heel and raced toward it. Even in her panic she couldn't help noticing that Mrs. Odom, who never seemed to walk farther than her own mailbox, dashed right past her, a bucket under each arm. And Randy's dad was hobbling along at a surprising speed, also bearing a bucket. But when she got to the Spencers' house, the entire house was already engulfed. Flames seemed to be bursting out of every window.

Still, without planning or discussion, as more and more neighbors arrived, a bucket brigade had begun.

Two lines of people stretched far down the road, all the way to the river, each person from the first line passing a bucket of water to the next, the last person tossing the water onto the blaze. The second line passed the empty buckets back to be refilled from the river. Even children helped, filling buckets from wells and troughs in the nearby yards.

"Did the family get out?" Mrs. Winston asked Mrs. Hawkins, both still wearing their kitchen aprons. "All them children! Are they safe?"

"My husband ran to make sure, but I think that's them gathered down the road there," Mrs. Hawkins replied, pointing to a huddled cluster in the distance.

Stella could see Mrs. Spencer, a frenzied look on her face, with Hannah and at least half of her siblings, huddled together, staring at the inferno. Stella couldn't begin to imagine what they were going through.

"They gonna have some mighty big needs come morning," Mrs. Winston said, glancing at the women in line beside her. They nodded with understanding. She passed a bucket to Stella. Stella's eyes went wide—she was being included with the women! She wedged herself into the line and passed the bucket on.

"Where's that blasted fire company?" Mrs. Bates asked in exasperation, heaving a sloshing bucket to Mr. Malone, who had just run up to join them.

He wiped his forehead. "They're not coming," he told them. "Y'all know them firemen are volunteers, and y'all know they're all white. When Gloria called, they just laughed at her and said they were too busy." He spat angrily in the dirt.

The bucket being passed to Mrs. Bates nearly slid out of her hands. "That can't be!" she cried, catching the bucket at the last minute.

How can anybody be so mean? Stella thought in fury as she swung the heavy pail to the next person.

Stella's parents came rushing up with Jojo, his eyes so huge Stella caught the reflection of the fire in them. She left the line for a moment to run to her mother.

"Are you all right?" Mama asked, her voice cracking, reaching for Stella. As her father assessed the scene, Stella could almost read his thoughts.

"It was the Ku Klux Klan, Papa!" Stella whispered hard.

"I know, baby. Tony told us," he said tightly. His face

steamed with anger. "They didn't hurt you, did they?"

"No, but they . . . they told me to warn you. One of them said something about a dragon. Papa, I'm so scared!"

"My sweet girl," her mother whispered over and over, hugging her so close that Stella could hardly breathe.

She broke away from her mother's embrace. "Papa, Dr. Packard was one of the riders. I'm for sure."

"Not surprised," Papa said gruffly.

"That fancy saddle. I'm sure I saw it that night," Stella added.

"Me and the men—we got a list of those we suspect are Klan—Packard's name is on top." Her father glared at the burning house.

"We could be next," Stella's mother said, grasping his arm. "It's the *Klan*, Jonah!"

"Give me one of them buckets," Papa cried out, shaking her arm loose, heading for the part of the line closest to the flames. Stella and her mother joined in farther back.

Though it was increasingly clear that the fire was winning the fight, Pastor Patton, his face smeared with soot, kept calling out, "Keep the water flowing, brothers and sisters!"

There wasn't any way to save that house, Stella knew, and wondered why they kept up their efforts. But then she realized that the fire was inching beyond the house onto the lawn. Several men with shovels had begun another line, heaving dirt from the Spencers' front yard onto the flames that were creeping into the grass.

"Over here!" Mr. Winston yelled. "It's spreading!"

Mr. Spencer darted in and out, thanking everyone, giving them dripping-wet rags to cool their faces, bringing dippers of water, weeping all the while. "God bless you all," he murmured over and over again. "God bless."

"All your children, they're safe, Hobart?" Stella's mother asked.

Mr. Spencer paused and wiped his forehead with the back of his hand. He blinked, his face a mask of disbelief. "We'd just finished supper. Butter beans and bacon. The children were scattered—doin' chores, homework, playin'. Just an ordinary evenin', you know. Then everything went black and red and smoke and screams." He covered his face with his hands.

Stella had never seen a grown man cry.

"But you gathered all your babes, right?" her mother prodded gently.

"Yes," he replied with a deep sigh of assurance. "The older children helped. We left everything, grabbed younguns, and ran."

"Where's your family now?" Stella's mother asked.

"My wife's just brought half of 'em to the Malones' kitchen, praise the Lord. And Mrs. Grayson's got the rest at her house, doin' her best to keep the little ones calm. Bless that woman," he declared before breaking away to help with the shoveling.

Shoulders aching, Stella kept her hands tight on each bucket passed to her until the next set of hands took it away. A huge roof beam groaned and collapsed. Those closest to the fire jumped back as a spray of sparks rose up like demonic fireflies, but the bucket brigade pressed forward again as soon as the embers settled. It seemed to Stella that every single person from her side of Bumblebee was trying to save the Spencers' house.

Randy and Tony stood together, pouring sweat, keeping perfect pace with the adults shoveling dirt.

There was a welcome cry of success—they'd just stopped the spread on the left side of the house! But that one spark of triumph faded when Mr. Bates, his voice cracking with anger, bellowed, "So we just gonna let them do this to us, burn our homes, scare our babies?"

"What we got to fight back with?" his wife asked helplessly.

"It's been like this since my granddaddy was a boy," Mr. Winston said.

"Then maybe it's time to make some changes," Pastor Patton suggested in a measured voice.

"Changes! This is all 'cause you and Hobart Spencer and Jonah Mills went to register to vote," Mrs. Odom fumed, thrusting a finger at the preacher.

"So Hobart and Harriet get their house burned down? Is that right? What's next—a lynching?" Mrs. Bates jerked the bucket from the woman next to her.

"I've seen a body swingin'. Three times in my life," her husband said, his voice low.

For a moment, except for the roaring of the smoky flames, everyone went quiet. Stella wondered how silence could be so loud.

✸ 28 ✸
The Hidey-Hole

Blisters were coming up on Stella's hands. She focused her concentration on not dropping a bucket. How could water weigh so much? So she didn't notice how many more people had joined their ranks, not until one of them held out a ladleful of water. She jerked her head up and nearly did a double take. The person offering her the ladle was white. Stella looked around. There were at least eight, ten white folks here! And jogging up with a pair of shovels was Mr. Jamison, the owner of the lumber mill. Merrill Bobbs, the man who sold fishing bait by the river, had somehow rolled a huge barrel of drinking water all the way from his house and was struggling to right it. "We ain't all Klan," he was saying to Dr. Hawkins, who rushed over to help him heave the barrel up.

"We know that," Dr. Hawkins assured him. "We know." The doctor darted in and out of groups of people, checking to see that no one was inhaling too much smoke, insisting that others rest or drink some water before letting them go back to fight the flames.

Stella blinked in the smoky darkness. For a moment she was sure she saw Dr. Packard's daughter Paulette standing behind the water barrel, but she couldn't be sure.

For certain she saw Mr. Stinson and his wife Fannie, lugging over a big pot. Mr. Stinson drove the postal RFD wagon that delivered the mail, so he knew and talked to everybody in the entire town, regardless of their race.

"Oh, my heavens, what a terrible thing!" his wife said, hands on her cheeks, gaping at the fire. "We brought soup, but oh Lordy, Lordy."

"Have a sip of this soup, Mrs. Hawkins," Mr. Stinson called out to Tony's mother. "We don't want that pretty singing voice of yours messed up with all this smoke!" She took it gratefully.

Patrick O'Brian, owner of the general store, hustled

up next, arms laden with jars of thick green pickles and bottles of Pepsi-Cola. Mr. Spencer twisted the lids off the pickle jars, while Mr. O'Brian passed out the colas. Just as they had with the buckets, folks took a sip of the soda and handed the bottle to the next person in line. Stella couldn't help but hope there'd still be some left by the time the bottle made it way down to her.

So when it did, still icy cold, she had a moment of happiness—two inches left! Pepsi-Cola was a treat Stella rarely got to try. Mama didn't see the sense in buying a drink when you could get it free from the well or a cow. But oh! The fizz. The crisp, clean frostiness. She desperately wanted to guzzle down those entire two inches, but she thought of her mother sweating beside her and took only the smallest of sips.

"Here, Mama, finish it up. I'm not that thirsty. I just had some water," she declared, handing her the bottle.

"You sure now?" Mama said.

Stella nodded, and her mother raised the bottle until the last drop was gone. A moment later she gave her head a shake. "Glory be—this Pepsi-Cola must be liquid sugar. Why, I do feel better!" She laid the empty bottle on the ground and reached for the next bucket of water with renewed gusto.

Mrs. Cooper from the candy store and her daughter, Thelma, arrived next, stepping into the bucket line and asking how to help. "Pass water and pray," Stella's mother replied.

Stella made room for Thelma, who took the bucket from Stella's now throbbing fingers and passed it along. Quietly they worked. There was nothing much to say. It was now fully apparent that nothing could be saved. The fire had been successfully doused on the left side of the house, but what remained was charred and smoking—the rafters glowing like skeletons in the night sky. Yet nobody seemed to want to put down the buckets.

Suddenly Mrs. Spencer came sprinting toward them, waving her arms wildly. "Stop!" she screamed. "Everybody stop! I can't find my Hazel! Has anybody seen Hazel?"

Mr. Spencer dropped the last of the pickle jars. "She's not with the schoolteacher?"

"NO!" his wife wailed, clutching his arm. "I was bringing the older ones over to Mrs. Grayson's house so they could help watch the little ones, and Hazel wasn't there! Mrs. Grayson said she thought Hazel was with me! *But I don't have her!*"

Mr. Spencer spun around. "Hazel?" he bellowed. "Anybody got Hazel?"

"Hazel? Hazel!" Mrs. Spencer shrieked desperately.

Mr. Spencer slammed the lid on the water barrel and leaped on top of it. "Does somebody have Hazel?" he bellowed.

No one answered. No one had seen Hazel.

"Hazel! Come to your daddy, Hazel. Hazel!" her father yelled. "Hazel? Where are you?"

He leaped off the barrel and ran through the crowd, checking every child he saw. Others dropped buckets and shovels to join his search, dread and panic thickening. Suddenly the back timbers of the house caved, letting loose a wall of heat that seemed like it would smother them all. But Stella felt the opposite of hot— she felt icy cold with fear. She envisioned Hazel running terrified, seeing her house on fire, running. . . .

She thought of all the secret passageways, of the halls and closets, of the tiny, added-on rooms in the Spencer house, of all the spots a small, frightened little girl could hide. Oh Lord, no! What if Hazel had chosen to hide in one of those? Why, Hazel had been talking, just the other day, about how she liked to hide.

Hide . . .

Hide! Hidey-hole!

Stella grasped Thelma's arm. "I gotta go do something. Distract my mama, just for a minute, okay?" she begged.

Thelma looked at her quizzically but recognized the urgency in Stella's request and agreed.

Stella turned to her mother. "I'll be right back. I gotta pee!" She broke from the line just as Thelma began asking Stella's mother a question. Stella ran as fast as she could around the flaming house to the backyard. "A hidey-hole!" she kept whispering.

The picture Hazel wanted to draw—what was it exactly? Think, Stella think! A huge brown tree, some blue water, and a sun with little red rays coming out of the corner. With a hidey-hole for a little girl. Where could it be? The picture wasn't much different from what most first graders drew, except the tree the child had drawn had a hidey-hole in it.

Stella headed for the woods, trying to think like a six-year-old. A girl that young wouldn't go very far from home. She'd be scared of the dark forest and afraid she'd get in trouble if she didn't hear her parents when they called.

So Stella peered carefully into the shadows, her only light the flickering remains of the burning house. She stumbled over the roots of a massive, eighty-foot oak that towered above her and landed on her knees. She started to pick herself back up when something occurred to her. The tree's roots, thickly twisted and fanning out like huge, grasping fingers, snaked out from its base.

Snakes! Hazel said her hiding place had snakes!

Stella got back down on her hands and knees. "Hazel? Are you in there, honey?"

Silence.

"Hazel? Hazel? It's all right. It's me, Stella. Don't be scared, baby girl. I'll take you to your mama."

A wee little voice called out from inside the labyrinth of roots, a tangle that had, Stella now saw, a hidey-hole in its center. "There's red fire everywhere! I'm *not* coming out!"

"I know, Hazel. But it can't hurt you. I promise. Come on out now."

A tiny head, hair going every which way, poked out from the roots. Hazel. Oh Lord, thank you Jesus! Hazel! Hazel was crawling on her hands and knees toward her. Stella kept coaxing her forward, then pulled the girl into her arms. She'd never felt so relieved in all her life.

"Let's go find your daddy and mama," Stella told her soothingly. "They've been looking for you."

✦ 29 ✦
Calling Your Name

Mr. and Mrs. Spencer couldn't stop thanking Stella and exclaiming to her parents. "I thought I'd lost the world when my house went up in flames, but Lord have mercy, that didn't mean *anything* compared to when I thought I'd lost my sweet baby girl!" Mrs. Spencer went on, Hazel still clutched in her arms.

"I can rebuild a house," Mr. Spencer added, "but our Hazel . . ." His voice broke, and he gave Stella what had to be his twentieth bear hug.

Stella's own parents couldn't stop touching her shoulders, smoothing her hair, brushing off her dress. She tried to shrug it all off, but when Tony sauntered over, simply to say, "Impressive!" before heading back to help with the final cleanup, she couldn't help but beam.

Now that Hazel was found, the fire was contained, and the house was clearly a loss, a number of folks wearily started making their way home. Some, however, stayed behind to toss one last layer of water and dirt on the smoldering remains.

"You know we're all gonna help you rebuild, Hobart," Papa told Mr. Spencer. "Every one of us."

"We're mighty grateful, Jonah," Mr. Spencer replied. He looked so very tired.

Stella's father had more to say. "Since my mama passed on last year, her house has just been sittin' there empty. I want you to head on over there for tonight, for as long as you need. It's small, but it's got a solid roof."

Mr. Spencer's face flooded with gratitude as he murmured his thanks once more.

It was after midnight by the time Stella and her family dragged into their house, bone weary and covered with soot. But when Stella finally got most of the ash and smoke off and fell into bed, her sleep was troubled. She tossed and turned, dreaming about dragons and ghosts, about fire and water, about snakes and hidey-holes.

★ ★ ★

Sunday morning came too soon, but their little church was packed. Families who usually came only for holidays filled the pews with scrubbed and subdued children. Men who usually skipped church to go fishing, and men who stayed late at the local bar and slept in on Sunday mornings, squeezed themselves in with the rest of the community.

Just before the first note of the first song rang out, the Spencer family, all fifteen of them, made their way down the center aisle. Their clothes were the same soot-stained ones of the night before, but every face was scrubbed clean, every chin held high. Hazel was wedged between her parents. As they walked past, every single person in the church stood and applauded. Once the family was seated, Mrs. Hawkins raised her arms for the choir to begin. The song she chose was, to Stella's mind, perfect. "Hush."

"'Hush, hush,'" the bass and tenors sang first. "'Somebody's callin' my name.'"

The altos joined in. "'Hush, hush, somebody's callin' my name.'"

Finally the sopranos. "'Hush, hush, somebody's callin' my name.'"

Then everyone together: "'Oh my Lord, oh my Lord, what shall I do?'"

The next verse was sung with deep, growling passion. Stella joined in loudly.

> *"I'm so glad that trouble don't last always,*
> *I'm so glad that trouble don't last always,*
> *I'm so glad that trouble don't last always,*
> *Oh my Lord, oh my Lord, what shall I do, what*
> *shall I do?*
>
> *Hush, hush, somebody's callin' my name,*
> *Hush, hush, somebody's callin' my name,*
> *Hush, hush, somebody's callin' my name,*
> *Oh my Lord, oh my Lord, what shall I do, what*
> *shall I do?"*

When Pastor Patton finally came up to the pulpit, Stella could tell every single person there was wondering what he would say. He began with a prayer.

"Dear Lord, You have seen us through good times and bad, through adversity as well as triumph. We thank You that no lives were lost yesterday, that You saved every member of the Spencer family. Houses can be rebuilt. People cannot."

A chorus of amens moved through the church.

"Sometimes we're not sure which path to take, whether it is time to fight, or time to wait. Help us to make the right decision, Lord, and help us to stand with nobility, no matter what, and to live without fear. Amen."

He looked across the pews. "Is it possible to be scared and brave at the same time?"

Stella scrunched up her forehead, not sure of the answer.

The pastor walked away from the pulpit, closer to the congregation. "I was fixin' to preach about David and Goliath this morning, because David was young, and brave, and faced an enemy who seemed to be impossible to defeat. But I changed my mind. This morning is too important."

Stella picked at a hangnail, but for the first time in many Sundays, she tried to pay close attention.

The pastor continued. "We sang this morning about somebody calling our name. That song is about listening to the voice of the Lord, about being ready when we are called."

Jojo elbowed Stella and pointed to his left foot. A thin line of brown ants was crawling across his big toe, and he was trying not to giggle. Stella clamped her hand over her mouth, stifling her own snickers.

Without warning, the pastor called out loudly, "Stella Mills, please stand up! I'm calling your name!"

"Huh? What'd I do?" Her heart thudded as every last person turned to look at her. She touched her hair, positive it was a mess, and wondered if the pastor had seen her laughing at the ants.

"Get up, Stella," her mother urged, nudging her.

Slowly Stella stood. In the center of the fifth row of pews, she stood, nervous, wondering what was going on.

"*This* young person is going to be the subject of my sermon today," Pastor Patton said.

Stella's knees nearly gave out. "Me?"

Her parents looked just as dumbfounded.

"Stella Mills is eleven years old," the pastor continued. "But she represents all the children here today—her own brother, the children of the Hawkins family, the Winstons, the Bateses, the Malones. Little Claudia Odom. All the families with children—too many to mention them all. And all thirteen of Brother

Spencer's brood—which is practically a small town in itself!"

Out of the corner of her eye, Stella caught Tony and Johnsteve and Randy pointing at her and grinning. She wanted to disappear under the floor.

"Yes, this little girl represents all of us. She is youth. She is promise. She is the reason we get up each morning and go to jobs where we are underpaid or mistreated, to work in fields that are dry and parched and refuse to yield. She stands there for *all* our children."

As Stella gaped at him, she sensed her mother sitting up a little taller, her daddy, too.

"Yesterday, in the midst of the heat and the flames, Stella Mills showed absolute bravery and courage as she ran *toward* the fire to rescue little Hazel Spencer."

Stella blinked. She didn't think what she had done yesterday was brave or courageous at all.

"And now, Hazel Spencer, stand up," the pastor said. "Stand up, honey. Now I'm calling *your* name."

Stella was relieved when all eyes moved to look at Hazel, who stood up and gazed around with as confused a look as Stella imagined she herself had on her face.

"Because of Stella Mills, Hazel Spencer is with us this morning. Because of Stella Mills, we know what bravery looks like. Because of Stella Mills, we give thanks that this child is with us. Because of Stella Mills, we know why we must keep on believing in our future."

Please stop talking about me and making me seem like something I'm not, Stella felt like screaming.

"I want all the children to stand now," Pastor Patton said. "All of you, get up! We value you. We honor you. We sacrifice for you. We're calling your names!"

As Jojo got up, a bright-blue marble clattered noisily to the wooden floor and rolled away. Mama shot him that *how dare you?* look, but he just grinned sheepishly and stood with the rest of the children. Stella was mighty glad to be joined by the others. They all looked from one to the other with pleased satisfaction.

"We promise to teach you, and to guide you," Pastor Patton told them. "Each of you is a David, and you *will* face many Goliaths in life. The job of the adults is to prepare you. And we will."

The grown-ups in the church started to clap and

cheer. Then they all began to stand as well, and hug their children, other folks' children, and even one another.

"Come to the front, children," Pastor Patton called out above the cacophony. "Come and sing for us. Mrs. Hawkins, will you lead them in "'Get on Board'?"

Stella and the others moved uncertainly to the front of the church. But Mrs. Hawkins took control right away, moving the group quickly up to the stage, placing the little ones in front and the taller ones in the back. She gave the signal to Mrs. Grayson at the piano, then lifted her arms, and the children began to sing.

"The gospel train is a-comin'
I hear it close at hand
I hear that big train movin'
And a rumblin' through the land

Get on board, little children
Get on board, little children
Get on board, little children
There's room for many a more

I hear that train a-comin',
It's comin' round the curve
It's loosened all its steam brakes,
And straining every nerve

Get on board, little children
Get on board, little children
Get on board, little children
There's room for many a more

The fare is cheap and all can go
The rich and poor are there
No second class on board this train
No difference in the fare

Get on board, little children
Get on board, little children
Get on board, little children
There's room for many a more."

Mrs. Hawkins led them though a dozen verses, each one faster and more spirited than the first. By the time they got to the final verse, the children were clapping in rhythm, the grown-ups were singing with them, and Stella could tell that the whole church was filled with a joy that hadn't been there when she walked in.

∗30∗
Church Ladies

Stella rode home with her family in a daze, not sure what had really happened. She heard a loud droning sound and glanced up.

"Look, Stella, look!" Jojo said, pointing. "An airplane!"

"Well, that's the cat's pajamas," Mama said, shielding her eyes.

Papa pointed as well, but in the opposite direction. "I'm lookin' at that eagle, flying low and slow. I 'spect he's not happy about an airplane takin' over his space."

Stella watched the eagle circle and glide, and thought back to Spoon Man's story.

"I bet you felt like you were gonna pass out at

church," Jojo teased her once both the airplane and eagle had flown out of view.

"I almost did!" Stella agreed. "But then you dropped that marble, and folks looked at you instead."

"About those marbles . . . ," Mama began.

Papa interrupted gently. "Leave the boy alone, Georgia. Today is Stella's day. I get a good feelin' right here when I think about what you did, Stella girl," he said, tapping his chest.

"'Cause she didn't upchuck or faint?" Jojo asked.

"No, silly. Because she was brave."

"But I really wasn't, Papa," Stella insisted. "I just figured out where Hazel was hiding."

"Ah, but you pushed away your fear in order to figure, that's what you did," Papa said. "Speaking of which, I think the preacher did a fine job getting rid of the anger and fear this morning."

Mama drummed her fingers on her knees. "But he never really gave any answers about what to *do* about the Klan."

"There are no answers," Papa said. "You just gotta keep goin' for your family, like the pastor told us. Sometimes bravery is just doin' what you gotta do."

They weren't home five minutes—Mama hadn't even had time to stoke the fire—when Dusty began to growl. A knock on the door followed. Dusty jumped up, barking fiercely. The dog didn't recognize whoever was at the door. Stella, alarmed, ran to quiet him, but he broke away, his hair standing up in stiff tufts on his back.

Her father swung the door open while Stella grabbed the dog more tightly this time.

"How do," Papa said in his deep voice.

Stella tiptoed behind him to see. She didn't recognize the two mousy white women who stood there.

Clearing her throat, the first woman practically squeaked as she said, "My name is Annie Lou Summers, and we are looking for Mrs. Mills. We heard, well, we heard, um, that she could direct us to the Spencer family."

"And I'm her sister, Mary Lou," the second lady said, hardly speaking any louder. "We are here from the Bumblebee Baptist Church."

Stella's mother hurried over to the door. "Come in, ladies," she said cordially. "Don't let our dog frighten you. We just got home from church services ourselves. Please come and sit a spell." Her mother offered them both a chair at the table. "Would you like some sweet tea?"

"Oh, you're very kind, but no, thank you," the ladies said almost at the same time. "We will be leavin' directly." They glanced nervously from corner to corner. Stella wondered what they thought of their house, then decided she didn't care.

The first woman, Annie Lou, told Stella's mother, "We heard about the terrible fire last night, and the women of our church decided we want to help that poor family whose house was destroyed."

Stella's first thought was to wonder if they knew any of the Klan members. She figured they probably did, probably went to church with some of them. Then she chastised herself for thinking mean thoughts—after all, these ladies were here to help.

Mary Lou added, "We've brought food, plus we have collected a pile of clothes for the children. And some pots and dishes and aprons for the lady of the house. It's all sitting out front in our automobile."

"Mrs. Spencer will be very pleased," Stella's mother said graciously. "It's mighty kind of you all."

"We'd like to do more . . . all those children. . . ,"

Mary Lou said, looking as if she wasn't quite sure what to say. "We just wanted to make sure they wouldn't, um, they wouldn't be offended, um . . ."

Stella almost smiled at their discomfort, but her mother filled in smoothly. "The Spencers will be very thankful for whatever you and the kind women of your church have to offer."

"The ladies decided they would try to be a blessing to the family, because of, uh, because of . . ." Now Annie Lou's cheeks blushed bright pink.

Stella started wondering what she would feel like in *their* living room.

"Well-a-mercy, we hear there are *thirteen* children!" Mary Lou finished for her sister, who was now fanning herself with her handkerchief.

"That's true," Stella's mother confirmed. "Would you like to meet them? They're staying in a house right next door for now. I'll walk over yonder with you."

"Oh, thank you, thank you kindly!" Annie Lou said, standing up quickly. Both she and her sister looked extremely relieved the conversation was over.

"These here are my children, Estelle and Jonah," Mama said.

"Would you two like to join us?" Annie Lou asked.

Stella and Jojo were at the door before the words were out of her mouth.

"Can we, Mama?" Stella asked.

"Yes, but leave the dog here. And mind your manners!"

"Yes, M'am."

"We'll help you ladies tote stuff," Jojo told them.

"Why, thank you, young man," Mary Lou said, smiling.

Stella wasn't going to pass up this opportunity. "Uh, do you think there's a chance we could maybe have a ride in your motorcar?"

"Stella!" her mother said sharply. "I'll have none of that!"

But Mary Lou seemed to understand. "I'll make sure you get a ride down the road before we leave," she whispered as they whisked out the door.

Stella was in heaven.

31
Riding in a Car

After she helped her mother wash and put away the dishes, Stella curled up on her bed and pulled out her notebook. Her family paid no attention to her scribblings, and Stella surprised even herself—today she could hardly wait to write down what had happened.

RIDING IN A CAR

Two white ladies let me and Jojo ride in a car today. Miss Mary Lou said it was a Model A. Nothing in Bumblebee smells that rich—nothing. I kept my hands balled into fists so I couldn't ~~axidently~~ accidentally touch the wrong thing and get it dirty.

Jojo ~~touched~~ ran his fingers over everything. He even rolled the window up and down with the knob on the ~~side door~~ passenger door.

It roared. Loud enough so that everyone on Riverside Road could hear. They all came outside to see us. Dust blew up around us as Miss Mary Lou stepped on the gas pedal and ~~galloped~~ zoomed down the road. She even blew the horn! It sounded like "Ga-OOH-uh. Ga-OOh-uh!"

I wonder if ~~cars~~ automobiles will ever replace horses and buggies. Some people say so, but I don't think it can happen. How can a fancy car go through the fields and help a farmer plant or pick?

And what would all the horses do?

⋆ 32 ⋆
Winners and Losers

All week the donations trickled in for the Spencer family, coming from the Riverside Road folks, as well as from the larger community. Another white church in Bumblebee sent a couple of boxes of goods, as well as both Negro churches in Bumblebee, and even one in Spindale. Clothes, food, bedding, shoes—everything a family could need—was thoughtfully and quietly left for them on Stella's porch or at the doorstep of what was once her grandma's house. Even building supplies started to pile up. Nails. Tar paper. Plaster. A sawhorse. Hammers and other tools. Wood. Wood. And more wood.

As another stack of two-by-fours landed by her porch, Stella couldn't help but think about how folks had come together when Spoon Man showed up. This time, however, they managed to do a cook-up for a whole house! Nobody had everything, but everybody had something to offer.

Mrs. Spencer knocked on their door several days later, a good-size box in *her* arms. "Mornin', Georgia," she said, setting the box on the table. Stella, braiding her hair into cornrows, came close.

"Good morning, Harriet," Mama said. "Have a cup of hot coffee."

"Oh, thank you kindly, Georgia, but I won't be but a minute. I'll take you up on that coffee another mornin', for sure." She started opening the box. "I've been sortin' through all the wonderful donations, gettin' the children ready for school, and I realized something."

"What's that?" Mama asked.

"Folks have been wonderful," she said, lifting things out of the box. "But even with my brood, we're gonna have more than enough. So I'm glad to be able to give as well as take—here are some things for Stella and Jojo."

Stella eased herself up to the table, her eyes

growing wide and wider still as Mrs. Spencer pulled out one, two, three, four dresses, looking to be just Stella's size, and two pairs of leather shoes, along with assorted trousers and shirts for Jojo.

"Shoes!" Stella exclaimed. "Shoes, Mama! Can I wear them to school? And new dresses, too! Oh, this is better than Christmas!" When her mother, beaming, nodded, Stella slid the black pair with the dark laces on her feet. They were a perfect fit. "Oh, boy! I'll be able to run so fast in these!" she exclaimed. "Thank you, Mrs. Spencer. Thank you so much!"

"I figured those would be about your size," Mrs. Spencer said, smiling as she watched Stella dance around the room. "You deserve something pretty."

Stella's mother grasped Harriet's hands. "I can't thank you enough, Harriet. Blessings out of tragedy. Imagine that."

Mrs. Spencer's smile grew wider. "There's one more thing down in the bottom of this carton," she said. "Could you help me lift it out, Stella? It's a mite heavy."

"Yes'm." Stella scurried over to help, delightfully aware of the clatter of her shoes on the hardwood floor.

When she looked into the box, she inhaled sharply.

"What's that you got there, Harriet?" Mama asked.

Stella slowly pulled the awkward object from the box. "Oh my! Oh, Mama!" she gasped. "It's a typewriter!"

Mrs. Spencer explained, "I'm not sure who donated it. But we have no need and no room for such a thing, and, well, you helped Hazel with her story, so I thought perhaps you liked to dabble in writin'. I hope you can make good use of it. A bit of writing paper came with it also."

Stella was struck speechless, until her mother gave her a *be polite!* look, and she managed to say, "Thank you *so* much, Mrs. Spencer! I never used one of these before, but I'm gonna do my best to figure it out."

"I'm glad," Mrs. Spencer replied. "We can never repay you for what you did for our Hazel, but it sure makes me happy to see the joy on your face." She turned to leave, but not without grabbing Stella and hugging her fiercely. Stella could barely breathe— Mrs. Spencer was not a tiny woman—but she hugged her back with equal measure.

"So, whatcha gonna do with that?" Mama asked after Mrs. Spencer was out the door.

Stella ran her fingers gently over the round black letter keys, pressing the *S* for Stella part of the way down, watching the type bar rise up toward the roller. Her mind was racing. Was this what newspapers used? She thought about the clippings in the cigar box—and shucks, even the papers on the wall—and thought, maybe . . . maybe . . .

Could I? Would this help? she wondered.

"You think what I write is good enough?" she asked her mother.

"What I think don't matter," her mother said, holding up and then refolding Jojo's new shirts. "Now get on out of here before you're late."

At school that morning, each of the Spencer children showed up with a fresh, clean outfit, and wearing an amazing assortment of new shoes. And it seemed no one could stop talking about the fire.

"That was the scariest sight I ever seen in all my born days," Herbert Spencer said.

"You're only ten. How many days have you been around?" joked his brother Hugh.

"It was cold that night, but the air was so hot," Carolyn remembered, rubbing her arms.

"I cried," Claudia admitted.

Stella sniffed the air. "I can still smell the smoke—it's like it's painted the whole town with that gray, choking smell."

"I've still got the smell in my hair and ashes under my fingernails," Randy said, looking at his hands.

Jojo mused, "Who knew we had so many buckets sitting around here in Bumblebee?"

Helen Spencer sniffled a little. "All my books got burned up," she said sadly.

"But I didn't," Hazel said quietly.

"And we are very glad of that!" Helen told her sister, grabbing her hand and squeezing it.

At last Mrs. Grayson cleared her throat and called the children to attention.

"Saturday night was a terrifying experience, children," she began. "We have all been touched in some way by what happened."

Claudia raised her hand. "Why are some people mean and some people nice?"

"I don't rightly know," Mrs. Grayson admitted. "But my job is to teach all of you to be the best people you can be."

Herbert made a fist. "You sure I can't punch any-body in the knee, for payback?"

Stella could tell Mrs. Grayson was trying to stifle a laugh when she said, "Sorry, but no, you can't do that."

Now Hazel raised her hand. "If my daddy builds us another house, will the bad men burn that one too?"

Mrs. Grayson paused. But then she said deliber-ately, "No, Hazel. I feel sure that you will be safe in your new house."

Stella wasn't certain Mrs. Grayson felt as confident as she sounded. But how do you answer a question like that from a six-year-old?

"Did you choose the entries for the newspaper con-test?" Stella asked, trying to change the subject.

Mrs. Grayson's face lit up. "Yes, I did! I mailed them on Friday afternoon. Making that announcement was next on my list of things to do today."

"Hey, did my essay make it?" Tony asked. "It was called 'The Snake in the Garden of Eden,'" he added with a grin.

"It was more about the serpent than about Adam and Eve, Anthony," Mrs. Grayson replied with a smile.

"Though I must admit I've never really looked at that story from the snake's point of view."

"I think snakes are slick," Tony said, playing with the sound of the letter *S* as he spoke.

"Indeed."

"So whose papers did you choose?" Carolyn asked impatiently.

"Well, first let me tell you something," Mrs. Grayson began. "Everyone did a fine job. I value every single story and poem and drawing that was prepared by a Riverside School student, but as you know, I could only choose three to represent us."

Stella sat quietly, daring to be hopeful.

"Our high school contestant will be Helen Spencer, who wrote a clever story called 'Bucky and the Beaver.'"

Everyone clapped politely, the Spencer children especially pleased.

"Our middle grades' entry," Mrs. Grayson continued, "was written by Carolyn Malone. She wrote about the loss of her baby sister. Her essay is very brave."

Stella bowed her head. Her essay hadn't gotten picked. She knew it. She *knew* it. She just wasn't good enough. She was happy for Carolyn, but still . . .

"And our final contestant, representing our littlest people, is Claudia Odom, who wrote a sweet and funny poem she calls 'Cornbread and Cows.' Let's give Helen, Claudia, and Carolyn a big round of applause and wish them the very best in the competition."

Stella's arms felt as if she'd been toting watermelons all day—everything about her felt heavy and slow and glum. So she was really glad when everyone had stopped clapping and cheering.

Seemingly utterly unconcerned that his essay hadn't been chosen, Tony asked, "So when do we find out who won?"

"The winners will be announced just before Thanksgiving," Mrs. Grayson told them all.

"What's the prize again?" Carolyn asked with a tentative smile.

"The selected entries will be published in the *Carolina Times*"—Mrs. Grayson paused for effect—"and the first-place winner will receive twenty-five dollars!"

The entire class gasped. "You didn't tell us about the prize money!" Johnsteve said.

"I did that deliberately," Mrs. Grayson replied. "A

person should write for the love of language, not for financial gain. Your writing can be compared to a cake. The money is simply the icing."

"I sure do love me some icing!" Tony said, licking his fingers while his friends laughed.

"Twenty-five dollars!" Stella murmured. She was feeling so low she felt like she belonged *under* her desk. She could have helped her father buy seeds and tools for next year's crop, a couple of new chickens, or maybe that sewing machine for her mother! Then she stopped herself. Helen Spencer should win. Helen and her family had lost everything.

Stella closed her eyes, thinking of the rich chocolate icing her mother whipped up and slathered on a warm layer cake. For sure, the icing made all the difference, but Stella wasn't sure how to make her writing like creamed sugar.

⋆ 33 ⋆
A Patchwork of Memories

Mrs. Grayson rapped on her desk. "Enough about the twenty-five dollars. Look, we're all a little high-strung today. How about if we do a little storytelling instead of geography?" Sighs of relief came from every direction.

"Let's circle up on the floor." She adjusted the ash pan, stoked the fire, and closed the lid. Stella had to admit she was glad her teacher had closed the grate—nobody wanted to be seeing flames of any sort this morning. "Are y'all ready?" Mrs. Grayson asked.

"Yes, M'am," the children replied.

Stella glanced at Jojo, smiled, and tried to cheer herself up.

"How many of you have a patchwork quilt that your

mama or your grandmama sewed herself?" she asked.

Almost every hand went up.

"You know, children, quilts, like stories, are part of our heritage, part of our culture. Some quilts even *tell* stories. Our past is a patchwork of memories and tales. You all keep that forever tucked in your pockets, you hear?"

"Yes'm."

Stella thought about that. Each of the families in Bumblebee was sort of like a piece of a big old quilt—their very own patchwork already woven together.

"For example," the teacher went on, "the story I'm about to tell you was sewn into a quilt my own grandmother made, so it's very special to me." She paused and gave them a curious smile. "Did you know that African people used to have the power"—she paused—"to fly?"

"That's not possible," Johnsteve interrupted.

"It's a *story!*" Carolyn retorted. "Now be quiet and listen before she makes us do state capitals or something."

Mrs. Grayson continued, "Flying was a gift given to the people because they cared for the sky and the earth and the animals. Men would soar in the heavens each night, just to talk to the eagles. Women, who glided on streams of air, wove pillows from the clouds. Men taught their sons the secrets of flying, and women taught their daughters, so the knowledge was passed from ancestor to descendant. It was a glorious time."

Stella looked out of the window wishfully. Clearly the passing down had stopped long ago.

"But it so happened that a whole generation of the African people were captured and removed from their land. And in time, their memories faded, the memories of the glistening beauty of the great blue heron, the rosy pink feathers of the flamingo, the powerful wings of the red-necked falcon. And because of their bondage, the connection between parent and child, between elder and newborn was destroyed. And the people lost the knowledge of how to fly. Or so they thought." Mrs. Grayson halted for a moment and drank a sip of water from a mug on her desk.

"Don't stop!" Hazel said, leaning forward.

"Patience, little one," Mrs. Grayson said, then she continued. "Slavery was hard, children. The people had to work from sunup to sundown. They had to pick, cut, plant, carry, cook, clean, wash, rake, hoe, dig, clear, build, and more. Every day was a struggle. Every day was full of unhappiness and pain. There was no joy.

"Now it came to pass that a young woman was living on one plantation, a woman of strength, a woman with dreams. Her name was Zalika, which in the Swahili language means 'born to royalty.' She constantly looked to the sky. She was able to predict the moment the sun would peep above the horizon, and the instant the land would fade into night. She had named every cloud, even though no two were ever the same. She knew when the sky would pour down rain upon them, and when the sun would burn their backs. She memorized the flight patterns of the birds as they soared above, studying them every single day.

"One hot summer day the man who called himself her master got very angry with Zalika. He screamed horrible words to her. Zalika refused to respond. She gazed at the sky instead. That made him even angrier, so he got out his whip to beat her."

"Whip?" Randy asked. "I don't think I want to hear this."

"Let me finish, Randy," Mrs. Grayson replied. "Trust the tale."

Randy shifted in his seat, arms folded across his chest.

"So, on this day," Mrs. Grayson continued, "young Zalika, who had never known even one day of joy in her life, decided she would not be beaten again."

"Goodie," whispered Claudia.

"The man raised the cruel leather whip above his head. His arm trembled with rage. His lips twisted with anger. His eyes filled with hatred. But Zalika would not even look at him—her eyes were focused on the turquoise sky. The full force of the man's arm came crashing toward Zalika. The tip of the whip curled like a serpent's tail. And it crashed down, down, down . . . down upon the hard-baked earth. Zalika was gone!"

Even Stella's eyes went wide.

"The man who called himself her master looked around in astonishment," Mrs. Grayson said. "Then he heard peals of laughter above his head. Shrieks of joy. He looked up and saw Zalika in the sky. She was flying! She fluttered and floated and hugged the clouds she had named, and flung them toward the sun. And she laughed, oh, how she laughed!"

"The memories of the ancestors, long buried within her, had emerged majestically. The other slaves looked up to the sky and saw Zalika flying, and the memories came flooding back to them as well. 'Come!' Zalika said. 'Come with me!'

"And so they did. One by one, they looked to the heavens and their feet lifted from the ground, their bodies swayed in the breeze. One by one they shed the abuse and pain and enveloped themselves in the memories of the ancestors. Every single one of them took to the sky and drifted away. And they never came back."

Stella cheered and clapped at the end of the story with everyone else. Mrs. Grayson got up, stretched, and told the class, "Looks like it's going to be a good day after all."

Stella walked over to the window and looked out. The sky was so blue that morning. So very blue.

✳34✳

~~typeing~~ typing

this is my very first writting with the
~~typewritttter~~ ~~typeriter~~ typewriter I roll the
paper in carfully tap out each lettr and words
appear like majic on the page i have to hit
this handle on the roller and it moves to the
next line i am very slow and i keep ~~messsing~~
messing up

mama just showed me how to put a period at
the end of a sentense and how to do do capitol
capitaletters. Hold the shift key. Type a
ltter. Undo shift key. Type more.

where is the comma and the questionnn mark
found them,,,,???

How do you ~~fix~~ misteaks mistakes? theres no
eraser.

how do newspaper people do this?

People type whole books? Must take yearsss.

even though my essay did not get ~~piked~~
picked for the contest I ~~thimk~~ think my
writting is getting better.

But not my typeeing for ~~sore~~. sure.

⋆ 35 ⋆
Walking Up to Freedom Land

Tuesday, November 8, was brisk and cold. Stella's fingertips stung as she washed up quickly and dashed back inside to the warmth of Mama's fireplace. Her father was out in the barn, forking hay to the mule, taking care of the chickens for her, and milking the cow.

"I'm sorry I didn't get up in time to help you make the fire, Mama," Stella said, wrapping her fingers around a hot mug of apple tea.

"Doin' for my family is my job," her mother said simply. "Drink your tea."

"Is Papa gonna vote today?" Stella asked.

Her mother closed her eyes. "Lord, help us. Yes."

"Mama, what if . . . well . . . what if the Klan decides to burn down *our* house? Or . . . do something worse?"

Stella asked, trying to keep her voice steady.

"I have no idea. It's been spooky quiet since the Spencer fire. No threats. No midnight riders. It's the silence that scares me."

Stella clutched the mug tighter and blew on her tea. When her father burst back into the house in a rush of frigid air, Stella's mother jumped up.

"What's got you so itchy, Georgia?" Papa asked as he pulled his chair up to the fire.

"It's Election Day. My husband thinks he has to vote. Jojo has a cold. I ripped my best apron on a nail. I spilled the bacon grease. There are crazy people who want to hurt my family. Houses are getting torched. I worry about what my children will eat this winter. Take your pick!" she replied sharply.

"Honey, I'm sorry. I know it's rough. But I'm doing this for you, for Jojo and Stella, for all of us."

"Humph," his wife said, reaching for the broom. She began swiping it roughly across the floor. The *spotless* floor, Stella noticed. "Tell that to the undertaker!"

"I gotta do what I gotta do, Georgia."

"Why?" she pressed. "It's not like Mr. Roosevelt needs your vote. Everybody hates Hoover because of the Depression. The newspaper says Roosevelt can't lose."

"But I can," Papa replied softly.

Mama gave the floor a huge *thwack*. "Who knows what's gonna be waiting for you there at the voting place?"

"Georgia, this is how it's gonna be," her father replied firmly. "I gotta stand tall. I have a right to vote, a *right*, I tell you. And a responsibility."

Stella sat motionless, hoping they wouldn't send her out of the room.

Her mama gave the floor another wallop. "And who will stand for me and the children, for the rest of the mothers and babies of Bumblebee, when we are all alone?" Stella couldn't remember ever seeing her mother so angry.

"For once in my life, I must be a man," Papa replied. "I'd like to think I am standing up, along with Mr. Spencer and Pastor Patton, standing up for all of us. If I don't stand up, I feel like I'm crouching low. And I ain't gonna feel low no more." And with that, he walked over to his wife and pulled her into his arms, broom and all.

Mama leaned into him, sniffing back tears.

Jojo, who'd been outside with Dusty, came racing in then, yelling, "Hot diggity! Looks like there's no school today."

"Why not?" Stella asked with surprise.

"There's a bunch of folks outside. Look!"

Already on the porch were Mr. Spencer and Pastor Patton.

"Come in," Stella's mother said quietly. "You still gonna do this, despite what they done to you, to your family, Hobart?" she asked.

Stella expected to see fire in Mr. Spencer's eyes, fire like the flames that had made tinder of his house. Instead his eyes were soft, gentle, and brown like the earth. "I have to show them they didn't destroy me," he said simply.

"But—" Stella's mother began.

Pastor Patton interrupted her. "Besides, we'll be safe enough, Georgia." He led her out to the porch, announcing, "You gotta see this for yourself. Seems that we have quite an escort out here."

Stella walked out with them, and her jaw dropped. It seemed every single colored man, woman, and child in town was walking up the road and convening in her front yard.

Johnsteve was among them, bellowing, "Come on out, y'all! It's votin' day!"

"Can I go too, Mama?" Stella asked, grabbing a cardigan sweater. Hastily she laced up her new shoes.

"Me too?" Jojo chimed in, bouncing up and down. "I ain't sneezin' no more."

Mama touched Jojo's forehead with her palm. She hesitated, then sighed before hugging them both. "Go. Be safe. I'll be here prayin' for all y'all."

"Thanks, Mama," Stella said, hugging her back.

Jonah Mills enclosed his wife's hands in both of his. "Come with us, Georgia. Please. We need you. *I* need you."

Stella watched her mother's face soften. Then, wiping her eyes, her mother took off her apron, tossed it on a chair, and said, "So what we waitin' for?"

Papa picked her up and spun her around.

Stella and Jojo couldn't scramble out to join the others fast enough. As they walked down the familiar road and into town, more and more families joined them. Women in aprons and head scarves. Men in work boots. Barefoot children. The barber. The man who owned the bar. The undertaker.

They walked quietly, solemnly, with Jonah Mills, Hobart Spencer, and Pastor Patton in the lead. They walked.

Stella's mother and Mrs. Hawkins linked arms, whispering, maybe even praying. Stella couldn't be sure, but she skipped along with her friends, glad Mama had come along.

Randy walked alongside his father, who had swung himself into the line in spite of his crutches.

"You want to ride on the wagon, Mr. Bates?" Stella offered, pointing to the one horse and buggy that brought up the end of the line.

"No, child. I'm walking," he replied firmly. "Did you know Mr. Franklin Roosevelt has polio? Just like me. And he's gonna be *president!* So I'm walkin'!"

Mrs. Hawkins started humming . . . humming a tune that had to be a hundred years old, a slave song, maybe. It was Claudia and a few of the first graders who joined in first, just like they did at school. Gradually more joined in, Stella as well, joined in singing words that hadn't quite meant as much to her before as they seemed to at this very moment.

"Ain't gonna let nobody turn me round,
Turn me round, turn me round.
Ain't gonna let nobody turn me round.
Gonna keep on walkin', keep on talkin'
Marching up to freedom land.

Ain't gonna let no hatred turn me round,
Turn me round, turn me round.
Ain't gonna let no hatred turn me round.
Gonna keep on walkin', keep on talkin'
Marching up to freedom land."

As they walked, the singing grew louder. It seemed to Stella that the walking went a whole lot faster as they sang. Then folks began adding their own verses:

"Ain't gonna let no fire turn me round,
Turn me round, turn me round.
Ain't gonna let no fire turn me round.

Gonna keep on walkin', keep on talkin'
Marching up to freedom land.

Ain't gonna let no Klansman turn me round,
Turn me round, turn me round.
Ain't gonna let no Klansman turn me round.
Gonna keep on walkin', keep on talkin'
Marching up to freedom land.

Ain't gonna let nobody turn me round,
Turn me round, turn me round.
Ain't gonna let nobody turn me round,
Gonna keep on walkin', keep on talkin'
Marching up to freedom land."

Stella craned her neck to check the end of the group. "Gosh!" she said to Carolyn, "there's a line of folks stretched longer than I can see!"

When she turned back, she saw the polling location, which in Bumblebee was the sheriff's office, looming ahead. So did everyone else, for the crowd went silent and slowed. But her father, Mr. Spencer, and Pastor Patton continued forward.

The sheriff, a lanky, red-faced man named Amos Sizemore, stood in front of the door, arms folded across his chest. The three voters stopped in front of him, held their hats in their hands, and waited.

"Do you think he'll let them in?" Stella whispered to Carolyn.

Carolyn shook her head.

"What are they waiting for?"

"Hush up!" Mrs. Odom told Stella sharply, her finger to her lips.

Stella's pulse pounded. A blue jay squawked in the distance. Everything else was noiseless anticipation.

The sheriff stood, legs wide, glaring at the crowd. The sheriff glaring at them was nothing new. But what *was* new, Stella saw, was that everyone was staring boldly back at him, no eyes cast down. No one moved for a good five minutes. Ten. Fifteen. Twenty-five minutes of silence and waiting.

Then, incredibly, and for no apparent reason, the sheriff stepped aside. He did not say a single word. He did not make eye contact with the men in front of him. But he moved out of their way.

And Pastor Patton, Hobart Spencer, and Stella's

papa walked through the door and disappeared into the darkness of that office.

Nearly the entire Negro population of Bumblebee stood in the street, quietly waiting while the three men voted. Stella noticed something else and nudged Carolyn. Some of the white townspeople who had come to vote didn't leave when they were through voting. They stayed and joined the group standing outside the sheriff's office. Mrs. Cooper, the candy store owner. Mr. Bobbs, the bait salesman. Mr. Stinson, the mailman. The undertaker. And still, nobody said a word.

The sheriff scowled at the scene, then abruptly disappeared inside the office.

Twenty minutes later, just as Stella thought she was going to collapse with worry and anticipation, her father, the pastor, and Mr. Spencer emerged from the polling station, smiles lighting their faces. And *now* she saw what she'd expected to see earlier in Mr. Spencer's eyes. They were on fire.

✦ 36 ✦

Landslide

since i have this ~~typwriter~~ ~~typewritter~~
typewriter now, i will pretend to write a
~~newspapper~~ newspaper. i will call it

STELLAS STAR SENTINEL (finally ~~lerned~~ how
to make all capitls. still cant fix messups.
This thing needs to be able to ~~erse~~ ~~eras~~
erase.)

Franklin Delano Roosevelt is the new
~~prsident~~. he won in a landslide. Landslide
makes me think of rocks and dirt falling down
a mountain. Not sure what that has to do with
an election.

but maybe it does. my papa voted. He is
a pebble. Lots of ~~pbbles~~ pebbles make a

landslide, right? his vote ~~countd~~ counted.

Roosevelt will move into the ~~white house~~ White House and will have a fine suppper to celebrate, i guesss. papa had cornbread and buttermilk and beans with his ~~freinds~~ friends at my house. i bet papa enjoyed his ~~cellebrattion~~ celebration more.

⋆ 37 ⋆

A Soft Cinnamon Cookie

Stella had just cupped her hand around the last egg in the nest, the chicken huffing and fluffing its feathers, when her father came into the coop on Saturday morning.

"Stella, your mama wants you to go get Doc Hawkins, and then run on over to the general store," Papa said. "Jojo still isn't feeling well."

"He's worse?" she asked. Come to think of it, Jojo had been coughing quite a bit at night. And he'd missed school yesterday.

"He can't keep anything on his stomach, and I don't like the sound of that cough. Mama says ask Mr. O'Brian for some Sal Hepatica and some of that awful-tasting Ayer's Cherry Pectoral." He reached into the pocket of his overalls and gave Stella two dimes and a nickel. "And ask Doc Hawkins to come by here first, please—before he makes his rounds. Your mama's pretty good with her liniment rubs and hot soup, but I want the doctor to check my boy, just for good measure."

"I'll hurry, Papa," Stella said, taking note of the worry on his face. She tucked the egg into the basket and handed it to him.

"You be careful, girl," he said. "No stopping at the candy store. No stopping to talk to friends. Straight there, straight back. You hear me?"

"Yes, sir," Stella said. And she took off.

Before she could even knock at Doc Hawkins's door, Tony opened it. "What you doin' out so early?" he asked with a big grin.

"Is your father home?" Stella asked, ignoring Tony's annoying cheerfulness.

"Yeah, he's out back getting the wagon ready. He's got a few patients to see today. Why?"

"It's Jojo—he's real sick. Papa asked if he could come as soon as he can. Can you tell him?" Stella said urgently. "I've got to go to the general store."

Tony's grin faded. "I'll have him there in five minutes." He disappeared back into his house, and Stella continued on down the road.

Her jumbled thoughts skittered like the marbles Jojo liked to play with as she made a beeline for town. Jojo had to feel plenty awful to be willing to stay in bed on a Saturday! She was so lost in thought that when she heard footsteps closing in behind her, she jumped. "You scared the life outta me, Tony! Where you going? Where's your daddy?" She pressed her hand against her thumping heart. It wasn't the Klan. It wasn't the Klan, she kept repeating to herself.

"Slow down. Relax. Daddy is probably already at your house. And I decided to come with you into town. Need to pick up something myself. Is that all right with you?"

"Sure, I guess."

"It's colder than a billy goat's butt today," Tony said, slapping his palms together. "You think we'll get snow?"

"Not likely. But winter is coming," Stella said, kicking up some of the crisp leaves along the road's edge.

"You worried about Jojo?"

"I really am. He's never, ever sick, so . . ."

"My father is a really good doctor."

"I know," Stella told him. She bit the inside of her lip for a second, then came out with it. "Hey, do you think folks think Dr. Packard is a better doctor than your dad just because he's white?"

"The white folks sure do," Tony said. "Don't know about the rest." He picked up an acorn and chucked it at a tree. "And what about you?"

"Your daddy—why, he's cured all sorts of ailments and problems in people around here! Remember when Randy Bates got the pneumonia? His mama thought he was gonna die."

"Yeah. My father stayed with him for twenty-seven hours straight. And remember the time Claudia Odom cut her foot on that broken glass? He sewed her up so good you can't even see the scar."

Tony leaped into the air, just reaching the lowest branch of a maple tree. He pulled off a handful of gold and brown leaves and handed them to Stella with a flourish.

She took them, smiled, then let the leaves drop. "So, you thinkin' on being a doctor like your father?"

"Maybe. That's why he lets me help him. Do you know I once saw a baby be born? I mean not a cow or a horse, but a real baby!"

"Golly!"

"Yeah, it was terrible and wonderful at the same time."

"Well, except for all the blood," Stella said.

"You know, it might sound odd, but I didn't even notice. When that baby first cried, I felt like a hero or something."

Stella huffed. "Well, the mother did all the work!"

"You're right about that," Tony agreed with a laugh. "What about you? You thinking about going into medicine too?"

"Not me! I *would* notice the blood." She stepped up the pace as they got closer to town. "I don't know what I want to be yet—gotta figure out what I'm good at."

"That makes sense."

The wind whipped at their backs as they approached the town square. Stella pulled her jacket tight. "Mrs. Spencer, she gave me a typewriter. I think as a thank-you for finding Hazel. Typing is really hard, but . . . this might sound strange, but I've got lots of stuff in my head, and when I'm hitting them keys, well, I get to thinking about how those newspaper reporters work, and I feel like if I keep at it, maybe I'll get not so bad, maybe I could do something like that." She paused, feeling silly, a little embarrassed she'd said too much.

"Good for you," Tony said, but she could see his eyes were on the candy store.

"I've got to get these things for Jojo, then get right back home."

"Tell you what," Tony said. "I've got a dime, so I'm going to get something chocolate. I'll meet you back here in five minutes."

"All right. Tell Mrs. Cooper I said hello."

At the general store, Stella pulled open the creaky front door. The bell jangled. Immediately she was overwhelmed by the smells of sweet cider vinegar, fresh sawdust, and cinnamon cookies. Her pace slowed. A barrel of pickles stood near the front door. Shelves of goods—buttons, handsaws, sugar, rifles, bullets, scissors, pencils, bolts of cotton cloth, medicine, toys, in no particular order—lined the walls. She could stay in the general store all day, just poking around.

She paused to touch a bolt of bright-blue cotton fabric. She closed her eyes—it was smooth and cool as she slid her fingers across it. *What magic Mama could make of that!*

"It's awful pretty, isn't it?" a girl's voice said.

Startled, Stella looked to see Paulette Packard fingering the cloth as well.

"It sure is," Stella replied, jerking her hand away and quickly remembering her mission.

"I've been wandering around for an hour, just buying little things, while my daddy sees patients. He said he'd have a dress made for me out of any fabric in the store," Paulette said, "but I told him I didn't need it." Her voice sounded a little sad, somehow, but Stella had no time to reflect on Paulette's problems—Jojo needed her.

"Well, enjoy your shopping day," Stella said, making her way to the store clerk as Paulette meandered toward the back of the shop where the homemade ice cream was kept.

"Hello there, young lady. How can I help you today?" Mr. O'Brian asked.

"Uh, my little brother is sick," Stella said. "He's got

a bad cough, an upset stomach, and a fever."

Mr. O'Brian looked genuinely concerned. "I'm sorry to hear that. Sounds like a touch of the flu. Some Sal Hepatica might help the young fella," he said. "It's a good product, but tell your brother to be warned. It fizzes going in, and fizzes coming out!" He laughed at his own joke, but Stella was in no mood for humor.

"Thank you," she said politely.

"And for the cough, you might try some Vicks VapoRub. It's got a little camphor and little menthol, and probably lots of other things they never tell us about. But it works. And Ayer's Cherry Pectoral is good as well."

"That's exactly what Mama asked for," Stella told him. "I won't need the VapoRub, though. Mama uses that stinky camphor oil." Stella made a face that made Mr. O'Brian laugh. "But I really appreciate your help. How much?"

"Let's see. The cough syrup is eighteen cents, and the medicine is thirty-two cents. That comes to fifty cents."

Stella fingered the two dimes and a nickel in

her palm. "I've got half that," she said awkwardly, flushing with embarrassment. She looked around self-consciously, but thankfully, Paulette was nowhere to be seen.

"Well, what do you know!" Mr. O'Brian said cheerfully. "I forgot to tell you—today is half-price day! And you have exactly enough."

Stella looked up at him. Their eyes met, and then she bowed her head with gratitude. "Thank you, sir," she said. "Very much."

"I hope little Jojo feels better," Mr. O'Brian said gently. He reached under the glass counter, pulled out a cinnamon cookie, and handed it to Stella, still warm. "My wife just took these from the oven. It's chilly today, and you've got a long walk home. This'll help keep you warm."

Almost in tears at his kindness, Stella thanked him once more and walked out of the store, the brown paper bag in her left hand, and the cookie in her right. She looked across the square for Tony.

"What you doin', gal?" a raspy voice said behind her.

Stella turned uneasily. Sitting on the bench in the front of the store were Max Smitherman and Johnny

Ray Johnson. They had not been there when she went in—she surely would have noticed.

"Girl, he asked you a question," Johnny Ray said.

"Just . . . just getting medicine for my brother," Stella replied, looking down at her shoes. Even though she could feel anger creeping up in her, she'd been taught since she was very young to say as little as possible to mean white people.

"Your mama know you spent her money on cookies for yourself?" Mr. Smitherman said, his voice taunting. "Or maybe"—he turned to Johnny Ray—"her daddy too busy votin' and such to be teachin' manners to his daughter."

"The cookie was a gift," Stella mumbled, the anger turning to fury.

"I'm thinkin' she don't need that there cookie," Smitherman said to Johnson.

"I'm thinkin' she musta stole that there cookie," Johnson said to Smitherman.

"Maybe she went in there and *voted* for the cookie," Smitherman said with a cruel laugh.

Johnny Ray, with two huge steps, was beside Stella. He snatched the cookie from her hand.

Stella could take no more. "You give that back!" she exclaimed. Even though she would never have put the cookie in her mouth now that he had touched it, she added, "You can't just steal other people's stuff!"

Johnny Ray stared her in the eye and stuffed broken cookie chunks into his mouth. Max Smitherman threw his head back and hooted.

Stella felt like her feet had gone frozen—she couldn't get herself to move away, but from the corner of her eye, she saw Tony running across the square. In seconds he was by Stella's side. "What's going on here?" he asked, grabbing her arm, looking from Stella to the men.

"Nothing. Let's just get out of here—now!" Stella whispered fiercely. They turned and started to walk away. Slowly.

Johnny Ray's voice stopped them.

"Wait just a minute, y'all."

They did not turn. Stella's heart began to thud.

"What you got in that there paper sack, boy?" Max Smitherman asked.

"Candy, sir," Tony replied.

"You steal it?" Max asked.

"No, sir."

"Where you get money to buy candy? Most a y'all can't even buy food."

Tony repeated evenly, "I didn't steal anything, sir."

"I don't believe you," Johnny Ray said. He grabbed Tony by the shoulder and spun him around. "Look at me when I talk to you, boy. I said, I believe you stole that bag of candy."

"I did not," Tony insisted.

Johnny Ray Johnson gave Tony a wan smile, then without warning, swung his arm back and punched Tony directly in the stomach. Stella screamed. Tony dropped to the ground, the bag of candy falling from his hand. Milk Duds rolled across the dirt.

Stella looked around frantically for a friendly face. Mr. O'Brian must not have heard her cry out—his door remained closed. Only a few people were in the town square that morning. No one turned to look. No one stopped to help.

"Get my father," Tony gasped. "Run!" At that, Johnny Ray kicked him in the side. Then Max's work boots connected with Tony's nose. Dark-red blood stained the dirt as Tony, grunting in pain, pulled his arms over his head to protect it.

Stella didn't hesitate. Mr. Smitherman blocked the door to the general store, so she flew across the square and burst into the candy store.

"Mrs. Cooper! Help!" she cried. "My friend Tony— he's getting beat up by grown men! Help him, please! I gotta get his father!"

Mrs. Cooper peered out the door with a gasp and shooed Stella away. "Run, child! Go get his daddy. I'll help him. I promise. Go!" She ran toward Tony, slamming the door behind her.

Stella ran. Faster than she had ever run on the playground, or with her brother, or in a school race. Stella ran. Her arms pumped in rhythm with her stride, her feet almost touching her backside as she sped back home.

She didn't think about whether she was running faster than Tony could or not, even his illegal runs on the track at the white school. She didn't think about what might be happening to him. She didn't think about whether she should have left him. She just ran. Sweat burned her eyes, but she did not slow her pace until she reached her house. Dr. Hawkins's wagon was still parked in front. Thank the Lord!

Breathless, she burst in the door. "Tony's hurt—in town! Beat up pretty bad," she choked out. "He's at the general store!"

Dr. Hawkins looked up in alarm. "Oh God, no! I'll see if I can borrow Mrs. Odom's car," he said. "Thank you, Stella." He rushed out of the house as Stella watched, torn between following him back to Tony and making sure Jojo was taken care of.

"How's Jojo?" she finally asked, still breathing hard. She handed Mama the package she had somehow managed to keep safe. She had actually forgotten she even had it.

"He's sleeping—feeling a little better at the moment," Mama said. "But, oh, young Tony!"

Papa opened the front door, took one look at Stella, and asked, "What the blazes happened?"

As Stella caught her breath, she told her parents everything. "Oh, Papa!" she wailed. "How will he ever forgive me? I just left him lying there on the ground—bleeding!"

Her mother smoothed her hair and tried to still

Stella's heaving shoulders. "You made the only possible choice you could have, considering the situation. You couldn't have done anything there, Stella. But you *got* him help!"

Her father added, "How were you going to fight two adult men who might have turned on you as well?" He grabbed his cap. "I'm going into town to help. Stella, you stay here and keep an eye on Jojo. Georgia, you might want to go be some comfort to Tony's mother. I'm sure Gladys will be full up with fear when she hears this news."

Mama and Stella looked at each other in agreement.

Before Papa left, he lifted Stella's chin. "Remember, Stella, you did the right thing."

Stella's eyes filled with tears. "So then why do I feel so bad?"

✦ 38 ✦

News Story

STELLA'S STAR SENTINEL

do I call this an ~~edton~~ edition? I guess I
can. It is my ~~newspper~~ ~~nrspapper~~ newspaper.

Headline: boy beat up in bumblebee

(I like using all those b's. gotta get
better at ~~capitols~~ capitals)

Written by: Stella Mills, reporter (I like
that)

Anthony ~~hawkins~~ Hawkins was attacked
yesterday in front of the general Store.
Two grown men kicked him and punched him and
knocked him to the ground. tony is tall for
his age, but hes ~~onlly~~ only eleven years old.

They said he ~~stolethe~~ stole the candy he

just bought. he told the men he had paid for
it, but they beat him up ~~anwy~~ anyway.

What kind of man thinks ~~its~~ it's fine and
dandy to make a boy bleed?

tony's father, dr. leroy hawkins, found him
in the back of the general store, bandaged up
by mrs. Cooper and mr ~~Obrian~~ O'Brian. my papa
helpd ~~thm~~ them back to ther house . nobody
else in town ~~helpd~~ helped.

Nothing was ~~brokn~~ broken except for tony
isnt happy and silly all the time like he used
to be.

This is my first real news story with a
headline. i wonder if anybody would want to
read this. i guess not. ~~everybdy~~ Everybody in
town already knows.

⋆ 39 ⋆
Willow Bark and Stinkbugs

Mama never missed church, but for the first time in years, she decided she would stay home with Jojo. Despite her dosing him with the cherry pectoral every few hours, and rubbing his chest with camphor oil, he had still hacked most of the night, sometimes having trouble catching his breath.

"I'm goin' out to the woods to fetch me some elderberries and mint to make this boy some tea—maybe a bit of willow bark too," Mama called to Stella as she pulled on a floppy hat. "You wanna come with me? Jojo will nap for another hour or so."

"Oh yes, Mama!" Stella replied right away. Papa had gone on to church, and she relished the alone time with her mother. She grabbed a jacket—the weather was sharp and biting.

Dusty, who usually was the first thing to whip out the door, simply lifted his head, then rested it once more on his paws. Since yesterday, he had left Jojo's side only long enough to eat or run out to relieve himself.

"I'll make some extra tea for Tony and take it to his mama," Stella's mother told her as they pushed their way through some brambles. "Willow is good for pain and swelling, and elderberry will halt an infection. I keep a little bit of elderberry at the ready."

"You sendin' healing stuff even though his father is a doctor?" Stella asked, curious.

"Can't hurt. Might help," her mother replied. "People been findin' and usin' healing herbs since forever."

Stella grabbed her mother's hand as they climbed over a log on the path. She kept trying to block out the memory of boots coming down on her friend's body. Then she remembered the silly leaf bouquet Tony had offered to her and wished she hadn't tossed it away.

"Tony's inside wounds are the ones that will be harder to heal," Mama was saying. "All the salve in the world can't cure what gets broken in somebody's soul." She gave Stella's hand a squeeze.

A cardinal, with a fluffing of wings, emerged from a nearby elm tree. *Flying.* Zalika, in that story, flew, Stella remembered. She wished Tony had had that same memory.

"You know who else was at the store yesterday, Mama?"

"Who?" Her mother stooped down to snap off a dark-green leaf. She sniffed it, nodded, and held it out to show Stella before tucking it in her apron pocket. "Arnica," she told Stella. "Makes a good salve for wounds, but not for tea. It'll hurt you if you eat it."

"I saw Paulette Packard. Looked like she was in the store spending her daddy's money."

"Hmm," Mama said, brushing aside some larger plants to get at a wispier-looking one. Mint.

"I'm mighty scared of her daddy," Stella admitted.

"So are we all, child."

Stella stooped to help find more mint. They were lucky to find it so late in the season. "You think white folks like that talk bad about colored people while they're eatin' supper?"

"I imagine they pay us no mind at all, Stella. I don't think we are important enough to them to be dinner conversation."

"Do you think Paulette saw what happened to Tony?" Stella sniffed at a leaf. Except for mint, she had no idea what she was looking for, but she wanted to show her mother she was trying.

"It doesn't really matter, Stella. Even if she had seen it, that girl didn't have much more power than you right then."

"I wonder if Paulette is gonna grow up to be mean like her father," Stella mused. "Or if people like Max Smitherman and Johnny Ray Johnson are gonna have children who hate us 'cause their daddies do."

"You think too much," her mother replied wryly. "And you can't blame the child for the father's sins." They headed closer to Kilkenny Pond and the woods behind it.

"Oh, look, Mama," Stella said, pointing. "Figs!" She hurried over to the fruit-laden tree, which had grown full and golden close to the pond. "Didn't we pick figs already back in June?" Stella happily gathered a couple of soft ones that had fallen to the ground. She *loved* Mama's fig preserves.

"Fig trees give twice a year," her mother explained, showing her a full branch. "Here, twist the fruit just a little, push it up toward that stem, and there you be!" The honey-brown fruit popped easily from the low-hanging branch.

"Pie tonight?" Stella asked hopefully.

"Next week for sure," her mother told her. She knelt close to Stella, then called out happily, "Ooh-wee! Look what I found—elderberries! These are surely the last of the season." As her mother plucked the purple berries, Stella coaxed a half-dozen more figs from the tree and placed them carefully into Mama's basket. Then she jumped backward, shaking her hands. "Ewww!" she cried. A half-dozen flat brown bugs— prehistoric looking—went flying. "Stinkbugs!"

"Mind you don't squash any," Mama warned. "You'll be washing your hands for a fortnight!"

"I stepped on a mess of them a couple of weeks ago. They stunk like a skunk!" Stella admitted.

"So *that's* what that smell was, stinkin' up my house!" Mama said, snickering. "Maybe when you be typin' on that machine of yours, you can write about *that*!"

Stella reached for a few more figs. "I, uh, typed something last night."

"I heard you click-clickin' down there at the table," her mother replied as she sorted the elderberries in her basket. "How's that goin'?"

"I had no idea how hard it would be. It takes me a real long time, and I mess up a lot. But it makes me feel mighty fine to see it all typed up. Even with all my mistakes."

"You keep at it, honeygirl. Just keep at it."

"Thanks, Mama." Stella plucked one of the dark-purple berries from the basket and lobbed it into her mouth. "Have mercy!" she cried, spitting and spitting and spitting. "My mouth is going to die! They're awful!"

Mama laughed out loud. "Elderberries make good wine, good jelly, and good medicine. But only bears eat 'em off the vine. I bet you'll never forget *that*!"

Stella spat again. "For sure."

"Let's start heading back," Mama said, still chuckling. "But first, I wanna grab a bit of that willow bark." She wandered over to a tree with deep, bowing branches. "Make sure the twigs are alive.

Dead bark, like these on the ground, won't work."

"How can you tell?" Stella asked, still sucking and smacking her tongue to get the bad taste out.

"If the twigs are bendy and the insides are green and wet, we've got what we need."

"Green and bendy," Stella mumbled, shaking her head, pulling at the branches, twisting them this way and that, peeling away at the bark. She tossed some thin shreds of bark into the basket, hoping she'd chosen correctly.

"Be mindful of snakes sleepin' in that dead wood, Stella," Mama warned. "Most of 'em just want to be left alone and won't even give you the time of day. But step on one, and you'll know real quick-like what time it is, that's for sure!"

Stella did a quick, dancing sidestep, looking down to check her bare toes. "Oh Lordy, Mama! Let's go home!"

"Good idea. We've got everything we need, plus a figgy bonus. Now we just need to boil the willow and the mint for twenty minutes or so, then let the tea sit awhile."

"We gonna put elderberries in it?" Stella asked dubiously.

"No. Those need to dry first. I'll be using those this winter."

"How do you *know* all this?" Stella asked, poking at the gathered bits in the basket.

Mama shrugged. "My mama taught me. I'm teachin' you. You will teach your daughter. Now, let's go check on Jojo."

★ 40 ★

Gifts

STELLA'S STAR SENTINEL

a ~~newspaer~~ newspaper with just one
reader--me

mama says some folks have ~~gifs~~ gifts, like
knowing which plants can heal and which ones
can hurt you.

Some ~~pepple~~ people have the gift of ~~writtin~~
writing i think I must of been sleep when that
gift was given out.

I ~~wundder~~ wonder how people who write real
good know what to say.

Im not even sure why I keep writing. Maybe
I should just stick to ~~reeding~~ reading.

I like the way books smell. I gues that is

strange. The pages feel good as I ~~tern~~ turn
them.

I wonder if there are books about
elderberries or figs in the library. I would
like to go to the library ands read the books
~~inthere~~ in there.

I would even wash my hands ~~afrst.~~ first.

⋆41⋆
Old Books and New Stories

A week later, just before Thanksgiving, Stella's classroom buzzed: A large box of books had just been donated to Riverside from Mountain View School. Tony, his bruises nearly healed, had insisted on helping carry the box to the center of the room. It was huge, and Stella could hardly imagine how many books were in there.

Excited, she picked out the first book, but she grew quiet as she saw how raggedy it was—the binding frayed, even missing pages. "I guess the Mountain View children got new books," she murmured.

Jojo, whose cough had finally faded, leaned over and picked out another book from the pile. "Oh, brother," he said with dismay, "this one's got scribbles all through it."

"What should we do with it?" Carolyn asked Mrs. Grayson, who was cutting out paper feathers for a turkey art project.

She sighed. "Let's make a pile of all the ones that can't be used. We can at least use them for kindling."

"Look here, though—a bunch of Hardy Boys books," Tony exclaimed, pulling a stack out of the box. "There's even a couple I haven't read yet."

"You see any Nancy Drews in there?" Stella asked, her excitement returning.

Tony dug a bit deeper. "Nope," he said. "Most of what's in here is"—he paused and opened the book in his hand—"outdated textbooks. Publication date on this one, 1919. Gee." He tossed it back in the box.

Stella's heart sank for a second time as she glanced out the window. The sky was like liquid steel. Heavy rain pelted against the tin roof of the school building. It was as if the weather was mimicking her mood.

A knock on the schoolhouse door broke up her dark thoughts—it was unusual for anyone to come in the middle of the day. Mrs. Grayson swung it open to find Mr. Stinson, the postal delivery man, standing there, water dripping from the wide-brimmed hat and dark-gray rain slicker he wore.

"Mornin'," he said, touching his brim.

"Come in, come in, Mr. Stinson, and get dry by the stove for a minute."

"That's mighty kind of you," he replied. "Too bad I can't bring in old Clyde," he joked, stepping in front of the potbellied stove. "He's not lovin' this weather one whit!"

Jojo, out of his seat once more, asked, "You like delivering the mail?"

Mr. Stinson placed a medium-size brown-paper package on the floor, peeled off his coat, and nodded. "Yep, I truly do, son. I'm probably the only person around here who knows just about everybody in Bumblebee."

"My mama loves when you bring us the Sears catalog," Claudia told him shyly. "Me too."

"My bag gets pretty heavy on catalog days. And around Christmastime, I guess."

"Don't you hate getting wet?" Randy asked.

"It comes with the job, son. But most days me and Clyde just take our time and enjoy whatever weather we get." He held his hands out toward the warmth.

Stella eyed the package. "We hardly ever get mail delivered to the school."

"Must be a special occasion then," Mr. Stinson replied with a wink. "Y'all wanna know something? I dropped a box full of shiny new textbooks to Mountain View School earlier this morning. But they didn't give me the royal warm-up treatment like you all. No sirree!" He picked the parcel back up and handed it to Mrs. Grayson.

"Thank you!" she said, fingering the twine circling it. "I have been waiting for this."

The postman wiggled his fingers in front of the fire once more, then picked his coat back up. "Well, I suppose I best be on my way. I ain't got no hankering to interrupt any more learning!" With that, he put his hat on, opened the door, and disappeared into the rainy morning.

"Is . . . is it what I think it is?" Carolyn asked, hovering beside Mrs. Grayson.

"It's simply the mail. That is all. Now sit down, Carolyn. In fact, everyone back to your desks," Mrs. Grayson said firmly.

Stella gnawed on her pencil as Mrs. Grayson put on her reading glasses, slid away the twine from the package, and snapped the wrapping open. One typed sheet of paper and several newspapers fell out; they looked like the *Carolina Times*. Stella watched the teacher read the letter, then pick up one of the papers. Mrs. Grayson read each page with careful deliberation, even stopping to take notes on an article she seemed to like. She allowed a hint of a smile to show on her face as she turned to the last page of the paper. Even though she knew she was not part of this competition, Stella switched to chewing on her fingernails. She glanced at Carolyn with a smile, with what she hoped was a look of encouragement.

Finally, finally, to Stella's immense relief, Mrs. Grayson looked up and took off her glasses. "Class, I have an announcement to make," she called out. But she hadn't needed to. Every one of Stella's classmates had been watching their teacher just as closely as she had.

"So, do you have the contest results?" Tony asked the question that screamed in everyone's head.

Mrs. Grayson smiled broadly. "I have some good news—something that honors us all."

"So what did they say?" Carolyn asked, raising her eyebrows at Stella.

"Here, I'll read you the letter," Mrs. Grayson replied, the corners of her eyes crinkling with pleasure. "'Dear Madam,'" she began. "'We would like to thank you for submitting the writings from your classroom. We feel that it is vitally important to support our Negro children in their educational endeavors. So, after reading selections from Negro schools all over North Carolina, we are pleased to announce that one of the winning contestants is from Riverside School!'"

Mrs. Grayson paused. The only sound was the steady patter of rain on the tin roof. *Why am I nervous?* Stella thought. *My essay wasn't even good enough to send in.*

Mrs. Grayson continued, "'The winning piece for the entire state is awarded a cash prize of twenty-five dollars and publication of the story.'"

Stella bit her pencil so hard it snapped right in half. Twenty-five dollars! *Oh, how Papa could have used that money!*

"'And first prize this year goes to'"—the teacher paused again, beaming—"'Helen Spencer for her delightful story, "Bucky and the Beaver."'"

Helen shrieked with joy.

The class hooted with celebration.

Stella looked over at Carolyn, who shrugged, then they both stood up and led the class in extra cheers for Helen.

"Wait! There's more," Mrs. Grayson said, shushing them. "'Thank you for letting us share her story. Please tell her parents that they should be very proud of Helen. We are enclosing several copies of the *Carolina Times* to share with the families in the Bumblebee community. Again, congratulations.'"

Stella blinked. She truly *was* glad that Helen would get the prize money—her family needed it for sure.

So why did she feel so low?

⋆ 42 ⋆
Two Small Puncture Wounds

The rain had stopped by the time school let out, but the road was a muddy mess. The bigger boys tossed wet dirt balls at each other, while the younger ones made mud snakes and threw them at the girls.

Stella dodged a slithering hunk of sludge. "Quit, Jojo!" she cried. "You throw one more thing at me and I swear I'll tell Mama!" She had taken off her new shoes and was walking carefully along the side of the road.

"I was sorta hopin' you coulda won that contest," Jojo said, falling into step with her. "I been wantin' a red-eye marble I seen at the general store."

Stella gazed down at her muddy toes. "My paper wasn't even sent in, Jojo," she reminded him. "Mrs. Grayson only submitted the best ones."

"Didn't you tell me you wrote about the Klan?" Jojo smoothed a huge dirt ball in his mucky palms.

"Uh-huh."

"You think maybe she didn't send your essay because it was too, too—I don't know—uh, dangerous?" he asked.

Stella stopped short and looked at her brother. "Gosh, I never even thought about that! You're pretty smart for a kid, you know."

"I know." Jojo made as if to fling the mud ball at his sister, but aimed for the third graders in front of him instead.

Stella looked up at the dark clouds still scudding across the sky. "More rain tonight," she commented.

"Good. More mud!" Jojo replied.

Dusty came tearing down the road to meet them, his sleek black fur mud-spattered. When he stopped, he shook his whole body from head to tail. Stella and Jojo jumped out of the way just in time to avoid a muck shower.

"Hey, boy!" Stella cried happily. "You come to meet us?"

The dog barked as if he understood, then ran ahead of them, urgency in his yelping and the rapid wagging of his tail, in the way he kept looking back to make sure they were following him.

"Dusty's acting peculiar," Jojo said, glancing over at his sister. At that, Dusty barked again and broke into a trot. Stella and Jojo jogged behind him. Once home, Stella leaped onto the front porch and flung open the front door. "Mama? Papa?" No answer. The house was empty.

"This morning Papa said he was taking the mule and going apple pickin'," Jojo remembered.

"Yeah, me and Mama are gonna start canning this weekend," Stella said.

"But where *is* Mama?" Jojo asked. The dog, his barking more insistent now, ran past the children and around to the back of the house.

"C'mon, Jojo," Stella said, dropping her shoes and following the dog. "Something's not right."

They chased after Dusty through the backyard, through the woods, and toward Kilkenny Pond. Bald cypress nodules and cattails hugged the water. Rocks and small sticks cut into Stella's feet as they ran.

Jojo spotted her before Stella did. "Mama!" he shrieked.

Their mother lay curled on the rain-soaked ground, not far from the jumble of dead willow branches, a mess of vomit beside her. Several dark-brown honey mushrooms spilled from her herb-collecting basket. As Stella approached, something moved in the undergrowth. Earth-colored. Was that a snake?

Stella felt an eerie calm come over her. She rushed to her mother and squatted beside her. She saw what had happened immediately. There were two small puncture wounds on her mother's left ankle. They bled just a little.

Stella turned to Jojo, who had started to cry. Slowly, carefully, she told him, "Go get Dr. Hawkins and tell him Mama's got a snakebite. It's *bad*. Then go find Papa—fast. You know where the apple orchard is. Run!"

Wiping his nose on his sleeve, Jojo dashed off.

Stella turned back to her mother, who was blinking slowly. Her breathing was uneven, raspy.

"I'm here, Mama," Stella said softly. "I'm gonna take care of you, you hear?"

Her mother's head moved imperceptibly. Then she licked her lips and murmured, "Rattler. Copperhead. Not for sure."

Stella looked back to the house. There was no way she would be able to carry her mother that far. She leaned close to her mother's ear and whispered, "I'll be right back, Mama. Don't worry."

With that she darted back to the house. She grabbed a couple of old towels, her father's Sunday necktie, a half-full bottle of whiskey that she knew her father kept hidden under his bed, a faded dress she'd outgrown, two blankets, and a pillow. Then she filled a bucket full of clean water, pumping that handle up and down so hard it was a wonder it didn't snap in half.

It took longer to get back, because the load was clumsy, the bucket was heavy, and she didn't want to spill. Her mother was lying just as Stella had left her, but she was trembling now. Her ankle was beginning to swell.

"Mama, I told you I'd be right back. I'm here now," Stella crooned as she lifted her mother's head and placed the pillow under it. "Did you know it's almost Thanksgiving, Mama? You were lucky to find mushrooms today, but you know all the secret places where the best stuff hides, don't you? You forgot what you told me about where snakes hide, I bet. I know I'm babbling, Mama, but I'm just tryin' to keep you awake till the doctor gets here, you hear?"

Stella first poured the cold water on the wound, watching as the oozing blood turned pale pink. Mama's eyes opened wide, registering shock, but Stella just kept rinsing the holes in her mother's leg.

"The next thing I'm gonna pour might hurt a little more," she whispered, "but I got to clean it best I can." Stella had no idea if she was doing the right thing or not. She was pulling from a gut instinct she didn't know she had.

She opened the bottle of whiskey, and as she sloshed most of it on her mother's ankle, her mother cried out in pain. Stella simply said, "Sh-sh-sh. It's gonna be all right." Mama stilled.

Stella held the pale-blue dress up to her face. Mama had made it for her when she was six. The cotton had been worn soft from dozens of wearings and washings. Without a second thought, Stella ripped it into wide strips, which she wrapped loosely round and round her mother's leg. She secured the bandage with her father's necktie, then bundled her mother in the blankets.

Stella soaked a piece of the torn dress with the last of the water and placed it gently on her mother's forehead.

There was nothing else she could do. So she snuggled under the blanket, wrapped her body close to her mother's, and held her tightly. It would be dark soon. *Where was the doctor? Where was Papa?*

She began to pray.

⋆ 43 ⋆
White Patients Only

"Oh God, Georgia!" her father exclaimed as he raced toward them at last. Jojo was not far behind, his face tight with worry. It was almost dusk.

Stella scrambled to her feet. "Papa! Mama's been bit. It's really bad." She looked around. "Where's Dr. Hawkins?"

"He ain't here," her father said, desperation in his voice. "He had to go out to Raleigh—medical conference. He's not due back for three days." Even as he spoke, he lifted his semiconscious wife into his arms, blankets and all, and strode back toward the house.

Stella grabbed the water bucket and hurried after him.

"Musta been a rattler," her father declared, moving

faster than Stella ever dreamed possible for someone carrying another full-grown person. "Canebrakes like to hide under wet wood in the fall."

"Mama wasn't positive," Stella told him, worry making her mouth dry. "I didn't see it. But maybe it *was* a copperhead," she added hopefully. "They're not so poisonous, right?"

"Still very, very dangerous," her father replied as he bounded onto the porch. Rather than try to carry her to the loft, he gently laid his wife on Stella's bed. Jojo ran to stoke the fire without being told.

"I didn't know what to do, Papa," Stella said, feeling her calm disappear and frenzy setting in.

"Girl, you done *so* good," her father said as he checked Stella's makeshift bandage. "I couldn't have fixed her up better myself!"

Stella hoped she'd done enough.

"Water," her mother whispered. "Water."

Jojo grabbed the bucket from Stella, ran to pump fresh water, and hustled it right back in. Stella carefully held a dipperful to her mother's parched lips, again and again, until Mama fell asleep.

"Jojo," Papa called out. "Run tell Mrs. Bates and

Mrs. Winston what happened. They'll know more than us what to do about snakebite."

Once Jojo rushed off, Stella turned to her father. "What are we gonna do, Papa?"

"I been thinking on exactly that. Your mother needs antivenom. Doc Hawkins is not gonna get back in time. I don't want to risk taking the wagon to Raleigh—you gotta keep a snakebite real still. The bumps and thumps could kill her, I believe." He stared at his work-worn hands. "I can build or fix anything with these hands," he said, his voice breaking. "But I can't fix this. Lord, I hate to say this, but we need Dr. Packard."

"Oh, Papa! There's no way he will come . . . is there?"

"Well, I doubt he would even answer the door if I knocked," her father said. "But you, he might just possibly listen to you. He's got a daughter about your age, don't he?"

Stella bit her lip, hard. "Yes, but he might be head of the Ku Klux Klan. Why would he help *us*?"

Papa dug his fingers deep into his hair. "He's got a wife he cares about. He's got a child he surely loves.

He's gotta know what it feels like to be crazy with worry for them." He placed his hands on Stella's shoulders. "Will you go, child? Will you try? Your mama's got maybe twenty, twenty-four hours."

Stella had never seen such desperation on her father's face. "Papa, I'll go. Don't worry. I'll go get Dr. Packard to come here and tend to Mama."

She headed up the road. That mile and a half to town never seemed so far away. She didn't run. Nobody would listen to a sweaty girl, she figured. The town square, almost deserted this late, looked very different at night. Buildings cast long shadows, and familiar shops looked foreign. She gazed up at the moon, which hung like a fingernail in the night sky. Light against dark. A sliver. A sliver of hope?

She did pick up speed as she passed the bench near the general store, even if no one was in it.

Dr. Packard's office, just around the corner, stood between the undertaker's office and the bank. Stella smacked her forehead. *What if he's gone for the day?* She hadn't considered that most shops closed up around four o'clock. She wondered if she dared go to his house. But then she saw with relief a light in the front window. An older white woman Stella didn't recognize, walking heavily on a cane, was just leaving the building.

"Thank you, doctor," she was saying. "I'm feelin' better already!"

Stella hurried to the door before it could close. "Good evenin', M'am," she said to the woman as she passed her.

"Humph," was all Stella heard in reply as the woman hobbled off.

Stella looked down and tried to smooth her wrinkled dress, suddenly regretting that she had not taken the time to change her clothes. She smelled of leaves and dirt and. . . she sniffed . . . and whiskey!

She had no choice. Just as Dr. Packard was closing the door, Stella pressed her hand up against it. "Uh, excuse me, sir," she began.

"What you want, gal?" the doctor said.

Stella hesitated. The doctor's eyes were such an odd color green—cold like fish scales. He was the only person she'd ever encountered with eyes just that color. She remembered those eyes peering from behind that hood on the day of the Spencer fire. She remembered those eyes from that afternoon so long ago when she'd been only five.

Stella blinked fast and shook her head. Then she blurted out, "My mother has been bitten by a rattle-snake! Copperhead, we think. . . ."

"So?"

"Please, sir, she needs a doctor. She needs antivenom. And she needs it fast."

"Y'all got a colored doctor down there. Don't be bringin' all this botheration to me."

"Dr. Hawkins is in Raleigh, sir."

"So go to Raleigh."

Stella bit her lip to quell her rising panic. "Mama can't be moved, sir. Papa says it would make the venom travel faster in her bloodstream."

"So now your pappy's a doctor? You don't need me." He laughed.

"Oh, yes, we surely do. I have a daddy and a little brother who love her very much. She's my *mother*, sir."

He shrugged. "She ain't *my* mama, so I don't rightly care."

Stella thought quickly, then dared. "I know your daughter, sir. We're the same age."

"Paulette don't know nobody the likes of you!" he sneered.

"But what if . . . what if it was Paulette or your wife that got snake-bit?" Stella asked, trying to reason with him.

He leaned toward her. "They got better sense than to get bit by a snake. Only stupid people let snakes bite them."

"Please sir. *Please*. Her leg is swelling. It's hard for her to breathe. She's barely conscious. Won't you be kind enough to come take a look at her? Please?" Stella implored.

"No! Now leave my property before I call the sheriff!"

Stella was stunned.

"But she might die!" she pleaded, blinking back tears.

"I told you—*I don't care*."

"Please," Stella whispered once more.

"Read my sign!" Dr. Packard said. Then he slammed the door in Stella's face.

Tacked on his door was a wooden plaque, neatly painted in red block letters. It said WHITE PATIENTS ONLY.

⭑44⭑
She Cried

When Stella got back home, she ran immediately to her mother, her eyes meeting her father's. She shook her head, and he bowed his. They'd known it would be a long shot. Neither of them had really expected Dr. Packard to come.

But Mrs. Winston *had* come. She called to Stella to get some vittles. "You must be starvin', girl."

Hot soup and warm biscuits appeared on the table. Stella hadn't realized how hungry she was. She ate it all. "Thank you, Mrs. Winston," she said gratefully. "Thank you."

Mrs. Hawkins began wiping Mama's brow with cold compresses. "I brought a pot of the same kind of elderberry-willow tea your mama fixed for my Tony," she said. "We been getting her to sip little bits."

"Is it helping?" Stella asked.

"Well, her fever ain't spiking, and the swelling hasn't gotten any worse, so that's a good sign," Mrs. Hawkins replied. But Stella could read the fear on her face.

Stella squatted by Jojo at the fire, where he was rolling two marbles between his palms, and pulled him close. Jojo rolled the marbles faster, and faster, and faster, and faster.

Finally he whispered, "Is Mama gonna die, Stella?"

"I don't really know for sure," Stella told him. "It looks pretty bad right now, but Mama is the strongest woman in Bumblebee, maybe in all of North Carolina."

"Uh-huh," Jojo replied. But he didn't sound convinced.

Papa knelt down beside them. "I'm gonna be honest with you two. If it was a rattler that bit her, that venom can be fatal. Depends on the type of rattlesnake, where the bite is, and the type of toxin it carries. We really don't know what bit your mama. But if it had been the most serious type, she'd already be gone."

Stella held Jojo tighter.

"But a person *can* survive a copperhead bite, if that's what got her. It ain't pretty, but it *is* possible. Antivenom sure would make it a lot less painful, and a lot more certain. Doc Packard coulda helped with that, but he didn't. So we're gonna depend on our friends to keep her comfortable, and our God to pull her through. Understand?"

They both nodded.

"Now say your prayers and get some sleep. We have some long days ahead."

Stella grabbed a quilt, covered herself and Jojo on his bed by the hearth, and began to pray. She prayed and prayed, listening to the embers crumble, certain she would never be able to sleep this entire night. So she was confused and disoriented when the front door burst open and several people entered, all seemingly talking at once.

Mrs. Odom, who usually dressed in demure long dresses and straw hats, had on a pair of men's overalls and an old plaid work shirt. Her hair was unstyled and all over her head. Stella could tell she'd left home in a real hurry. Her daughter Claudia, looking sleepy, wore a nightgown. And Dr. Hawkins—Dr. Hawkins!—in his Sunday-go-to-meeting three-piece suit and fedora filled the room with his authority.

Claudia spotted Stella. "Can I lie down with you and Jojo, Stella?" she asked, coming over. "We been in the car all night."

Stella hopped up, patted the place she'd been sleeping, and tucked Claudia in. Claudia was out before Stella even had the blanket fully around her. Then Stella ran over to the adults. Her father was in the midst of giving Mrs. Odom a bear hug. He pulled Stella into it.

"Stella girl! Praise the Lord! Mrs. Odom here heard about the snakebite, got in her car, and drove all the way to Raleigh to get Dr. Hawkins from his medical conference!" Papa told her, mashing them both.

Mrs. Odom extracted herself from the embrace, but her cheeks were flushed with pride.

Stella felt she was going to burst. Mrs. Odom? She *drove*? The woman who wouldn't ever take the car out for fear of getting dust on it? Praise the Lord indeed!

"And there's even better news!" Papa added, hope in his voice. "Doc Hawkins had some antivenom at his office. He's giving Mama her first dose right now."

"So Mama's not going to—I mean—she's gonna, she's gonna live?" Stella asked incredulously.

"Nothing's for sure yet," her father replied. "But at least she has a fighting chance now. And you know what else, Stella?"

"What?" Stella couldn't imagine anything more.

"Dr. Hawkins says that what you did out there in the woods was simply amazing. Cleaning and treatment of the snakebite the way you did probably saved her life, kept her alive long enough for him to get here."

Stella felt relief flood through her, and, for the first time since she'd found her mother, she cried.

⋆45⋆

Snakes

STELLA'S STAR SENTINEL

(maybe ill let somebody read this)

SNAKES

Reporter's Note: I am ~~typeing~~ ~~typingss~~ typing this while my mother recovers from snake bite.

Thankyou to all our ~~frends~~ friends in Bumblebee who brought food. And healing teas. And the cakes and pies--yummy

And to Mrs. Grayson who brought me a book on snakes.

What i learned:

-snakes are not mean. Mama ~~probly~~ probably stepped on it.

-some snakes are hatched from eggs. i did
not know that!

-~~simtoms~~ ~~symtoms~~ symptoms after being
snake-bit are pain and swelling and throwing
up. And thirstiness (is that a word?) and not
breathing ~~goo.d.~~ good.

-numbness and tingling in the face, and
stomach cramps. Mama has those also.

and her leg mightt be ~~damged~~ damaged for
good. that ~~isnot~~ is not good.

-antivenom is a gift ~~fromf~~ from god. And
the proper name is ANTIVENIN. I don't know
why. Spelling is hard enough without ~~docotrs~~
doctors changing things.

-Mama might have long-term ~~reslts~~ results
like pain and swelling and difficulty walking

-Mama is alive. Thank God.

⋆ 46 ⋆
Splash Scream Surprise

It was cold. Too cold for Klansmen to burn crosses. Too cold for nightingales to warble. Too cold for sitting on the steps. But Stella couldn't sleep this December night, so even though she knew her parents would disapprove, she'd tiptoed outside to think.

She took a walk on the banks of Kilkenny Pond, trying to ignore the nippiness of the night, the troublesome memories of Mama's ordeal. Despite her heavy woolen jacket, the cold still seemed to ooze into her bones. She figured it was about three in the morning. Nothing stirred.

The sky was so clear that the glint of stars, the glimmer of the moon shimmered across the pond. Occasional small circles radiated from the center of it. Stella stopped and watched, then looked to the heavens and gave a simple prayer of thanks. Mama now lived with a great deal of pain, but she lived. She lived! Papa had carved her a sturdy cane; the blisters and sores had mostly healed, the shortness of breath all but gone. Her leg remained swollen and discolored, however. Dr. Hawkins said it might get better, might not. To Stella it seemed a small price to pay to live.

Yawning finally, Stella turned back home. She hoped Jojo had remembered to bring in firewood; the logs had just about faded to ash when she'd tiptoed outside.

But before she had managed a pair of steps, she heard a splash, followed by a sudden scream. Concentric rings grew larger and larger on the dark water, then gradually disappeared. An owl hooted. The wings of birds that had been sleeping flapped in surprise.

Stella froze until the second scream came, this one louder, more desperate. "Help!" came a cry. "Help me!"

Stella moved toward the sound, toward the splashing and wild thrashing that followed another gurgled cry. "I can't swim! Help me!"

Trying to find the source of the scream, Stella raced around the bank of the pond, then stumbled to her knees. She looked to see what she'd tripped over. A pair of girl's shoes. Out a few feet, a pale arm extended from the water, reaching for the sky. A head bobbed up, momentarily, and just as quickly disappeared.

Stella didn't pause to think; she ripped off her jacket and plunged into the water, gasping as the cold grabbed her, soaking through her hair, a feeling she hated. *Mama's gonna kill me for messing up my hair,* she thought insanely, wondering at the same time why such a ridiculous thought had come into her head.

She swam hard toward where she'd seen the person go down. Stella could swim, but she preferred not to. Most colored girls she knew felt the same way—they didn't swim because it took a whole Saturday afternoon to get your hair pressed and braided, and it was just too much trouble to mess it up on purpose. White girls wouldn't understand.

The water was deeper than she expected, and oh, so very, very cold. Still, Stella swung her arms through the water, searching, searching. Her fingers were growing numb. Still she searched. Her feet felt like stones. She searched until she couldn't bear it—she had to get out or she'd die too. She propelled herself under one last time. And she hit something. Stella grasped at it—an arm! She pulled. The person dug their fingers into Stella's shoulder. Stella twisted away but held on to that arm. She kept pulling until a head—a girl's—popped above the surface, gasping and choking. The girl clamped onto Stella, grabbing at her, dragging them both down, thrashing, under the waters of Kilkenny Pond. Stella kicked and kicked, forcing them back up to the surface.

"Stop!" Stella cried when their heads broke the surface once more. "Stop or you'll kill us both!"

Sputtering and choking, the girl kept pulling at Stella's arms, hair, anything she could grab. "Can't swim!" she gasped.

"But I can! Stay still. Don't move! We're nearly to the shore." At this point, feeling more angry than frightened, Stella, with strong, sure strokes, slowly made her way to the bank of the pond. The girl clung to her desperately, but she stopped flailing while Stella made sure the girl's head stayed above water.

When her feet could feel the bottom, Stella heaved

the girl onto the bank. She was surprisingly heavy.

When at last Stella had her safely up in the grass, the girl's eyelids fluttered open. She looked around in alarm, then rolled over and threw up, water splashing everywhere. Stella helped her sit up, and, finding her own coat, wrapped it around the girl's thin shoulders. Her long blond hair was a tangled mess, and her blue eyes looked wild. It was Paulette Packard.

Stella stared. Dr. Packard's daughter! "Are you all right?" Stella finally asked. When Paulette nodded, teeth chattering, Stella asked, "What in blazes were you doing in the pond in the middle of the night?"

Paulette looked around in a daze, then buried her face in her hands and burst into tears.

Stella, mystified, let her cry, until she, too, was shaking with cold. "So, you decided to go for a midnight swim?" she finally pressed.

Paulette wiped tears against Stella's coat sleeve. "No," she said at last. "It's pretty obvious I'm not much of a swimmer."

"That's for sure."

Paulette pulled Stella's jacket tight. "You—you— saved my life!" she suddenly exclaimed, as though stunned by this realization. "Oh my goodness, you saved my life! Thank you. Oh, thank you!"

"Yeah, I guess I did," Stella said, her teeth now chattering. "Look, we have to get to my house," she added, "or we'll catch pneumonia or something."

Paulette hesitated.

"It's just down that path," Stella explained. She started to stand.

"Wait," Paulette said. "I need to explain."

Stella waited. Fatigue was quickly replacing the adrenaline. Her skin felt frozen. She wanted to go home. But she asked again, "So why were you in the water?"

"I like the pond at night," Paulette replied. "My daddy would tan me if he knew—it's a good piece from my house—but lots of times I just come to sit and think."

Stella thought about this, surprised. "Me too," she finally answered.

"Well, tonight I came out here because my parents were fighting—again. They never even notice that I'm gone."

"Does that happen a lot—the fighting?" Stella asked.

"Yeah. Pretty often." Paulette stared at the ground, her hair dripping around her face. "Sometimes it gets so bad I just have to get out of there." She looked up at Stella. "I like to write. Every once in a while, I bring a notebook out here and write about animals and stuff. Anything to get my mind off things going on at home."

Amazed, Stella asked her, "So why did you take your shoes off? It's freezing out here."

Paulette started crying again. "I was, uh, being stupid. . . . I thought maybe . . ."

"You didn't go in on *purpose*?"

"I didn't! I swear! Well, not really. But—I was just so upset! I figured if my daddy . . ." she dropped her head and sniffled. "If I got, well, sick with something really awfully bad like pneumonia or cholera or something . . ."

"You can't get cholera from cold water," Stella scoffed, crossing her arms.

"I know. I know. But I wanted to get sick with something really bad so he'd pay attention to *me* for a change! He's a doctor—if I had to go to a hospital or something, maybe he'd remember he had a little girl. Maybe my folks would stop fighting." She started to cry again.

Stella frowned. She wasn't sure how to react to the shivering white girl. How unhappy she had to be!

Paulette continued. "But the second my shoes were off, I changed my mind. And that's when I slipped. That's the truth. Golly, that water was so COLD!"

"Amen to that! It was butt-freezing cold. Plus, you almost drowned me!" Stella added, her whole body now trembling.

"I'm sorry. I'm so sorry! My father will be really angry when he finds out," Paulette said even more miserably.

"Not glad you are safe?"

"No, he'd first be worried I mighta told anybody what was going on at home."

"Your father is mean," Stella said bluntly.

Paulette raised her chin. "I know."

"He hit me once, when I was little. He made my mother cry."

"I'm really sorry, Stella." Paulette took a deep breath. "He's hit me, too."

"Really?"

"I've learned to stay out of his way."

Stella dug her toe into the muddy ground, but the

fury she felt toward Dr. Packard flared up, and now there was no holding back. "Your father . . . your *father* . . . wouldn't treat my mother when she got bit by a snake. He had some of the antivenom that could have helped her." She yanked the jacket away from Paulette and wrapped it around herself. "But he refused to share it with a colored lady."

"Oh no!" Paulette cried out. "Maybe I can talk to him about helping her in the morning. Even though he roughs me up sometimes, I know he loves me. He gives me money and buys me stuff." Water continued to drip from the ends of her hair.

But Stella did not care, not one little bit. She shrieked, "You don't understand, Paulette! My mother could have *died*! *Died*—do you hear me? It'd be too late for your daddy to do anything!"

Paulette's pale face went paler still. "Oh, Stella, I'm so sorry. Please forgive me. Please forgive my father." She climbed shakily to her feet and reached out her hand.

Stella backed away, too livid to stop. "Let me tell you something else about your sweet daddy! Your father is a member of the Ku Klux Klan! I saw him near this very pond, burning a *cross*. I saw him on the road after the Spencer house got burned down. I saw him. I saw *your daddy!*"

Now Paulette poked a toe in the dirt. "Don't you think I know? I watch my mother starch and iron that stupid white uniform every single week. He's prouder of that uniform than he is of us."

"Proud? People have lost their *lives* because of the Klan!"

"It's been like this all my life," Paulette confessed. "He's always ranting and raving about how awful colored people are. That's when he's not yelling at my mother and smacking her around."

This caught Stella up short. "He hits your mother, too?"

"All the time. She's really good at covering the bruises."

Stella didn't get it. "Why does she let him get away with it?"

Paulette shrugged. "He's the town doctor. He's got money in a town that's mostly broke. They get the best pew in the church, the best tee times at the golf club in Spindale. She's not about to give all that up and be a nobody."

"A nobody like me and my family?" Stella asked, the anger flaring again.

Paulette looked away.

"My mother almost died, will *never* be healthy again, and it's your father's fault!" Stella fumed. "I'm gonna tell."

Then to Stella's utter surprise, Paulette touched her shoulder and said, "I think you should."

Stella blinked hard. "I wasn't expecting you to say . . . that."

"I wasn't expecting you to save my life," Paulette replied, offering Stella her hand for the second time.

Stella hesitated, but this time took it. After a moment she said, "I'm gonna take you to my house. It's freezing out here. We gotta get out of these wet clothes and talk to my folks. They'll know what to do."

✦ 47 ✦

STELLA'S STAR
SENTINEL

THE ELEMENTS

Earth. Water. Air. Fire. We ~~lerned~~ learned
in science class that ~~anceint~~ ~~ancent~~ ancient
people used to beleive that was what life was
made of. i guess it makes a little sense.

Earth. Thats dirt. what farmers plant in.
Where people get buried. On a dare I ate
some dirt once. It ~~tastedd~~ tasted like ripe
potatoes.

Water. We need it to live. But we cant
~~breeth~~ breathe it. We can drown. everything
drinks water for life. i have even seen ~~burds~~
birds sipping drops of water from a leaf.
Water tastes like—like life

Air. without air, we die. it blows and
swirls sometimes, joining up with water to
make ~~sturms~~ storms. Air can move water, but I
don't think water can move air.

Fire. fire destroys. But without it, we
could not cook our food or warm ~~ourselfs~~
ourselves. I've never tasted fire, but the
smoke from it makes my mouth feel thick.

Truth. i think that is the last basic
element. Paulette would have died if I had
not been out there. I almost died too. That
water didn't care what color we were.

her ~~fatther~~ father is full of hate. She
knows that is the truth. So does every living
soul in Bumblebee.

so there is really nobody to tell.

★ 48 ★
Just Plain Joy

Stella was learning to run the kitchen. Mama, sitting with her leg elevated on a pillow, directed, guiding her on details Stella had never paid much attention to before—like boiling and frying and searing. Hot-water corn bread—cornmeal, water, flour, sometimes an egg—plopped into sizzling grease. Succotash—okra, corn, tomatoes, and peppers—sliced, diced, boiled, then fried. Cookies—sugar, butter, cinnamon, flour, and more sugar. Stella had generally preferred eating the goodies rather than cooking them, but Mama's years of gentle lessons were paying off now.

Jojo, without being told, had taken over most of Stella's barn chores. The family never missed church.

"Is it truly Christmas in two days, Stella?" Jojo

asked for the seventieth time. "And for sure we don't have to go to school this morning?"

"It truly is, Jojo," Stella assured her brother for the seventieth time. "Why do you think I'm making Christmas sugar cookies?" She wiped her hand across her forehead, smearing flour across her brow. "And no classes—just the pageant tonight. Now go get me some more sugar."

"I think there are a few raisins left in the jar," Mama called out, pointing to a high shelf.

Jojo looked at Stella's face and burst out laughing. "You got more flour on your face than in the bowl!" he cried.

"Keep that up and I won't let you have any of my cookies," Stella warned, flicking flour his way.

"You'll probably burn them again anyway!"

"You're right," Stella agreed good naturedly, "but I'm getting pretty good at this cooking thing." Jojo scurried to find the raisins. She sat down at the kitchen table to stir the thick dough.

"Stella, honey—I might not be fit for dancing, but I can certainly stir some batter," Mama said, stretching her arms for the bowl.

"But I *want* to do it," Stella said with a smile. "I'm gonna try to make us a really good Christmas supper, Mama. All by myself."

"I have no doubt. Holler if there's something you can't figure out."

Stella heard a rustling in the loft and hopped back up to get the coffee. Papa was awake. The family had seen him less and less the past month—in addition to keeping their farm going, he'd taken a part-time job at the mill to bring in a little more money, so he was often gone, and always tired. She poured the coffee into a cup and brought it to the table, but Papa strode directly to his wife and kissed her on her forehead.

"Mornin'," he said. "How's my Georgia Peach?"

"Fair to middlin'," she replied with a bright smile. "I'm just sittin' here watchin' our daughter cook like a grown woman!"

"Mornin', Papa," Stella said as he made his way to the table. She slid the steaming cup in front of him.

"And how's my other favorite girl?" he asked, slurping the coffee. "Don't tell your mama, but I think you might have learned how to brew the perfect pot of coffee!"

"I heard that, Jonah Mills," Mama said, laughing.

"Are you off work today, Papa?" Stella asked hopefully, now placing a slice of lumpy corn bread in front of him.

"No, but I'll get home early—in time for the Christmas pageant. And I'll be home Sunday. Since it's Christmas, they're closing the mill the whole day."

"Good," Stella said. "You can get some rest."

"Tell that to the cow, the mule, and the chickens!" her father said with a bemused smile. "Y'all ready for your show tonight?"

"You and Mama are gonna love it," Stella replied. "I get to be assistant director."

"That sounds like an ideal role for you. How you doin', girl?" Papa asked. "You gettin' enough sleep?"

"Yes, Papa. I'm feelin' just fine."

"You make my heart happy, Stella," her father said. "For everything you do with your brother, helpin' your mama with the cooking and washing. You have no idea."

"Everybody helps. The neighbors still bring food from time to time. Jojo has gotten really good with getting firewood and cleaning the barn and doing the outside chores. And Mama's gettin' so much stronger. We're gonna make it."

Her father gulped down the rest of his coffee and began lacing his boots. "I'll see you all tonight," he said. "Lookin' forward to seein' that pageant of yours." Putting on his hat and taking the corn bread with him, he headed out for the three-mile walk to the mill, where, Stella knew, he'd be lifting logs and sweeping sawdust all day long.

Mama dozed while Stella washed the dishes, swept the house and both porches, and peeled potatoes for supper. When Mama woke up, her eyes were glowing. "Hey, you two! Let's decorate the Christmas tree!"

Jojo jumped with excitement. "What we gonna put on it?" he asked.

"How about we start with popcorn?" Mama suggested. She told Stella to heat the butter, toss a half cup of the popping corn in, cover it, and wait for the pop.

"Pop! Pop-pop! Pop-pop-pop-pop-pop!" Jojo sang along with the popcorn as the kernels exploded into delicious bits of fluff. When she took the top off the pan, he cheered.

Taking a needle she'd threaded, Mama showed

them how to pull it through each piece of popcorn. Soon they had a long chain done. Then another. They would have had three, but Jojo kept eating the popcorn.

"What else? What else can we put on the tree?" Jojo asked, his mouth full.

Mama had an idea. "Go out to the henhouse, Jojo, and get some pretty feathers. Look for the long ones—the tail feathers! And pinecones! There must be a thousand pinecones—" He darted out before she finished speaking, leaving the front door wide open.

"Jojo! You don't live in a barn!" Stella called after him, only to hear her mother laughing.

"What?" Stella asked as she closed the door.

"You sound just like me!" her mother said.

While Jojo was out collecting, Stella had another idea. She pulled out a long spool of bright-red knitting yarn from Mama's sewing basket. She took every single spare button from the basket's bottom. As with the popcorn, she strung each one onto the yarn. She tied a knot between each button so they wouldn't run together. She had just knotted the last button when Jojo returned, triumphant, with the egg basket filled with feathers and pinecones. Together, they made a garland of pinecones and chicken feathers, so pretty that Mama decided then and there that they had just created a new holiday tradition.

Strand by strand, Jojo and Stella walked around the tree, wrapping it with the popcorn, the buttons, and the garlands. When they finished, all three stood back, Mama leaning on her cane, well pleased at how pretty it was in the fading afternoon light.

"I think it's our best tree ever," Jojo said, picking a popcorn husk from his teeth.

"Just plain joy," Mama breathed.

"We couldn't have done it without you, Mama," Stella replied, knowing in her heart it was true.

⋆ 49 ⋆
Not in the Script

From the back of the church, the children from Riverside School streamed in, their hands clasped as if in prayer. Some wore bedsheet or towel robes, others were in costumes made from feed sacks. As they made their way to the front of the church they sang, in voices sweetly in tune, thanks to all the practices,

"Away in a manger,
No crib for his bed,
The little Lord Jesus
Laid down his sweet head;

The stars in the bright sky
Looked down where he lay,

The little Lord Jesus
Asleep on the hay."

Stella, standing in front beside Mrs. Grayson at the piano, nodded, pleased. Perfect so far. Then a little voice shouted out, "Hi, Mommy!" Four-year-old Hope Spencer had taken her hands out of the prayer position to wave wildly at her parents.

"Hi, Daddy!" her twin sister Hester echoed, waving as well.

Stella put her finger to her lips, trying to shush the twins, but people in the audience simply chuckled, and Mrs. Spencer waved back, happiness splashed across her face.

"The cattle are lowing,
The poor baby wakes,
But little Lord Jesus,
No crying he makes.

I love thee, Lord Jesus,
Look down from the sky
And stay by my cradle

Till morning is nigh."

When they reached the front, the children scrambled to find their places. Tony, Johnsteve, and Randy, the three wise men, stood regally in one corner—for only a minute, however, because somehow, Randy's crown toppled from his head!

"Hey! My king crown!" Randy whispered far too loudly. The crown rolled off the stage and Randy rushed to retrieve it, dropping a jar of what was supposed to be his gift to the baby in the manger. Apple jelly, not frankincense or myrrh, spilled across the stage.

The other two "kings" clapped their hands over their mouths to restrain their laughter. Randy scurried back to his place, crown in hand. But as he tried to adjust it back on his head, he bumped into Johnsteve, who teetered on the edge of the pulpit. Tony grabbed him to keep from falling, causing his own crown to come tumbling off. The three boys gave up all attempts at dignity and now were just trying to keep from bursting into laughter.

"And it came to pass that all the people had to go pay taxes," Helen Spencer, as the first narrator, was saying in a loud and proper voice. Stella could tell she was trying to get the play back on track. "But Mary and Joseph couldn't find a hotel anywhere! So they stayed in a barn." Stella looked up in surprise when Helen added, "I bet Mary let Joseph know that she wasn't very happy about that either!"

That wasn't in the script. And now the whole audience began to laugh.

Then Carolyn, dressed in a long blue dress that had been donated by Miss Mary Lou of the Bumblebee Baptist Church, and a blue bath towel draped over her head like a shawl, added dramatically, "Joseph! A barn? Are you for serious? Don't you know I'm about to have a baby in a few minutes?"

Stella looked to Mrs. Grayson, who looked horrified. But as she scanned the audience, who was clearly enjoying it, she settled into a bemused headshake.

Hector Spencer, wearing his father's plaid bathrobe, played Joseph. He looked around for a moment in confusion; this was not how the play had been rehearsed. So he glared at Carolyn, glanced at his father in the audience, then said, crossing his arms, "I'm doin' the best I can, woman! Times are hard!"

By this time, the people in the pews were rolling with laughter, including, Stella saw, her mother. It made her feel so good to see her mother laughing.

The shepherds forgot the words to "Rise Up, Shepherd, and Follow." The little angels simply sat down on the stage giggling because Baby Jesus, played by Hetty, climbed out of the box that was being used for the manger and said loudly, "Mama! Gotta go pee-pee! Now!" Mrs. Spencer ran to the front and grabbed the child, but it was clearly too late.

At that, Mrs. Grayson gave up. Laughing herself, she said, "I think we better halt this production right now!"

She took Stella's hand and walked from the piano to the front of the church. "Ladies and gentlemen," she said, still laughing so hard she had to catch her breath, "the children worked very hard on the pageant this year, but as usual, it never quite goes as planned. We had a counting song for you, and a full-length play—really!"

Pastor Patton joined them, trying hard to suppress his own guffaws. "We all know how the story ends, folks. Jesus was born, gifts were given, and the world was made a better place. But you know what? I think one of the best gifts of all is laughter. There's never enough laughter. So let's thank our children for that. Please give all of them a huge round of applause!"

"We still gettin' presents?" Jojo piped up after the clapping subsided.

That made everyone laugh again. Mrs. Grayson replied, "Bags of fruit and candy for all of you are on the back table. Merry Christmas, everyone!"

Mrs. Hawkins, sliding onto the piano bench, struck up the chords on the old piano and ended the pageant with, "Go Tell It on the Mountain."

"Go tell it on the mountain
Over the hills and everywhere
Go tell it on the mountain
That Jesus Christ is born.
Hallelujah!"

★ 50 ★

Thinking About Flying

STELLA'S STAR SENTINEL CHRISTMAS EDITION

There is nothing more ~~butifull~~ beautiful
than dawn on Christmas morning. the sky is just
~~beginnng~~ beginning to wake up. Early morning
clouds cover the stars like blankets. The moon,
looking sort of like a ripe peach, hangs in the
sky like another ~~decoration~~ decoration.

(editor's note: wow! That was pretty good! I
just might be getting the hang of this writing
business.I just might glue this to the wall!)

(second editor's note: I am the editor! And
the reporter! I like that.)

For Christmas I wish for more love, less
hate. and more cookies.

soon all the ~~chickens~~ roosters on the lane,
who think they have more power than they
really do, will decide it is time to wake
everybody up. They don't know the sun will
come up anyway.

Roosters never look beyond the fence. I
doubt if they ever think about flying.

But I do.

Acknowledgments

Union Mills, North Carolina. Yes, this is for you. Thank you for the stories on the porches late on summer nights. Thank you for the lightning bugs and the sweet tea. Thank you for the memories you didn't even know you were creating.

Thank you, Lord, for the release from the black hole of "wordlessness" I found myself in a couple of years ago. I will never again smirk about the pain of not being able to find the right words. Sometimes they hide in deep, dark places. Thank you for the light.

Thank you to my editor, Caitlyn Dlouhy, for giving me the tools to work through the pain, for understanding and space and time, which in the world of publishing is a supreme and precious gift.

Thank you to my friend and agent Janell Walden Agyeman, for her strength and encouragement and complete belief in the power of the spirit, and the wisdom of the ages, and for her acknowledgment of the ancestors to hold us up and lead us onto our designated path of light.

Thank you to the National Association of Black Storytellers, who inspire me each year, and who taught me the nuances and subtlety of storytelling, the secret voice of the drummer, and how to weave our history into story, to weave culture into fiction.

Thank you to my parents for their continued complete belief in me, (Mom, your story is coming next—look out!), and to my husband and children and grandchildren for their love and support.